ABOUT THIS BOOK

Welcome to Havenwood Falls, home to sexy men, strong women, and neighbors who bite. Discover supernatural mystery, thrills, and romance in a place where everyone has a deep, dark, and often deadly secret. This is only but one...

Teeny Weeny Tahini lives a simple life in Havenwood Falls. Using her faerie magic, she serves up psychic readings and healing potions in her town square salon. In her free time, she collects herbs in the woods while keeping her tiny forest friends out of trouble. But trouble is exactly what the seven wee folk find when they come upon a maimed snow-white owl . . . and a mummified body nearby.

As Teeny doctors the owl, she's shocked to discover the fowl-shifter is her nephew Mathew, whom she hasn't seen in ages. He's been on the run for years, searching for sanctuary. How he became injured, though, remains a mystery—even to him.

For two decades, Shayin Pisik has been hunting the one thing she needs to be reunited with her betrothed. Her enchanted locket guides her to Havenwood Falls, warning that she must complete the ceremony started years ago under this week's Blood Moon, or she will forever be alone.

A disappearing body, another attempt on Mat's life, and suspicious stinky strangers lead Teeny to uncover the clever plans of a lovesick heart. But the winged must take on the wicked for true love to reign in this Teeny Weeny faerie tale, a quirky reimagining of *Snow White*.

THE WINGED & THE WICKED

A HAVENWOOD FALLS NOVELLA

T.V. HAHN
KRISTIE COOK

HAVENWOOD FALLS BOOKS

Forget You Not by Kristie Cook

Old Wounds by Susan Burdorf

Fate, Love & Loyalty by E.J. Fechenda

The Winged & the Wicked by T.V. Hahn & Kristie Cook

Alpha's Queen by Lila Felix

Ink & Fire by R.K. Ryals

Lose You Not by Kristie Cook

Tragic Ink by Heather Hildenbrand

Nowhere to Hide by Belinda Boring

Flames Among the Frost by Amy Hale

Rock Me Gently by Susan Burdorf

From the Embers by Amy Miles

Defying Gravity by Kallie Ross

Break Me Not by Kristie Cook

How the Dead Lie by Stacey Rourke

The Lurkers Within by Danielle Bannister

The Collector: Awakening by Kristie Cook, R.K. Ryals, Belinda Boring &
Nadirah Foxx

Addicted to You by Belinda Boring

Affliction Mine by C.J. Pinard

The Ward & the Wanderers by T.V. Hahn

Toil & Trouble by Melissa Wright

Of Salt and Stars by Seven Jane

Redefined by Morgan Wylie

Betrayal Among the Frost by Amy Hale

Forever Loyal by E.J. Fechenda

Fate's Demand by Emily Cyr

The Wu & the Wand by T.V. Hahn

A Demon's Redemption by JD Nelson

Also try the YA line, Havenwood Falls High; the historical paranormal line, Legends of Havenwood Falls; the darker, sexier side of town, Havenwood Falls Sin & Silk; and the local supernatural college, Sun & Moon Academy.

Stay up to date at www.HavenwoodFalls.com

BOOKS BY KRISTIE COOK

SOUL SAVERS

A Demon's Promise

An Angel's Purpose

Dangerous Devotion

Dark Power

Sacred Wrath

Unholy Torment

Fractured Faith

Genesis: A Soul Savers Novella

Awakened Angel: A Soul Savers Novella

Supernatural Chronicles: The Wolves (A Soul Savers Tie-In Novella)

Wonder: A Soul Savers Collection of Holiday Short Stories & Recipes

THE BOOK OF PHOENIX

The Space Between

The Space Beyond

The Space Within

In memory of my mother, Yvonne, who always believed I had talent, and always nurtured my "child-like" or one might say "pixie-like" qualities.

And to our readers, who we hope enjoy this quirky little tale as much as we enjoyed writing it.

CHAPTER 1

WHAT'S THAT SMELL?

*T*eeny Weeny Tahini swung her feet back and forth under her seat at a small table toward the back of Broastful Brew. It was a quiet coffee shop where the older folk—as well as those with private (perhaps even shady) business dealings—escaped the hustle and bustle of the larger Coffee Haven, the other purveyor of morning brews on the town square of Havenwood Falls. The diminutive woman pursed her lips and raised her teacup to her mouth, the steam from the hot liquid curling mysteriously around her head, as she watched her friend across the table.

In every way Teeny Weeny Tahini was petite, Mayor Barbara Stuart was large. Much like the Amazonian breed, with broad shoulders, high cheek bones, and a rather large bosom, Barbie possessed the perfect aura for a mayor: "I am not one to be reckoned with." Teeny, with her nearly black eyes and dark auburn hair, and Barbie, with her azure eyes and large bouffant that looked like lemon cotton candy, sat in stark contrast to one another. Yet they seemed a perfect fit. The kind of fit that came to longtime friends.

While they were neither old (by appearance, anyway) nor involved in shady business dealings, Broastful Brew had been their meeting place for many a decade, and likely would remain so as long as they were all around—Tahini, Barbie, and the coffee shop itself.

"So another Founders Day has come and gone, and for once, without a hitch," Tahini said as she placed her teacup back on the wooden table between them.

"Yes, it was quite uneventful," Barbie said with a mix of both pride and disappointment in her voice. While she strove to maintain peace and protect the best interests of the town, the mayor had a bit of a mischievous streak of her own. "Not even a peep of excitement at the library's ribbon cutting. The most exciting part of it all was the high school team, at least in the beginning. Then they lost their flair, too. At least we had the Blackstone family drama recently. That's been interesting . . ."

"And Ronan Bishop is back," Tahini said pointedly.

"Oh, yes." Mayor Barbie perked up. "You heard the gossip?"

Tahini raised a dark brown brow. "I don't need the gossip."

"So do you know what he's up to? Everyone's wondering where he's been and why he's back. But you know Ronan. Secretive as ever."

Tahini shook her head. "No, I do not know why, but I'll keep an eye on him."

"Anything else I should know, Madame Tahini?" the mayor asked her companion.

Tahini was fondly called Teeny Weeny Tahini by the townsfolk —a nickname that not only did she enjoy, but actually instigated decades ago when she adopted her pseudonym Madame Tahini. Once she decided to set up shop as a fortune teller, Madame McFeeny just didn't quite exude confidence or credence. Madame Tahini, or Teeny Weeny Tahini, waxed poetic.

She slowly closed her eyes and tipped her head back. Her nostrils flared open as she whiffed the scents that swirled and combined into the aroma of the Broastful Brew. She easily distinguished the dark roast Arabica beans from the sweet marshmallow scent of the vanilla ones piled in a large glass jar on the counter by the cash register. She inhaled deeply again, sucking the curling steam from her teacup into her nose. She appeared to be in a trance as the mayor patiently waited for her friend to come back, so to speak.

A few moments later, Tahini's eyes suddenly flew wide open, and the word "visitors" erupted from her mouth. Teeny had a sweet birdlike voice, like the chirping tweet of a mocking bird, but "visitors" came out of her like a deep, haunting growl. Barbie gasped in surprise and jumped back, practically falling out of her chair.

Mabel, Broastful Brew's owner, came rushing to the table. "Are both of you okay?"

Tahini and Barbie stared at each other for a long, silent moment, both with wide eyes. Then Tahini blinked, and Barbie cleared her throat.

"Teeny says we should be expecting visitors soon," the mayor finally answered.

"Well, that's fabulous. Business is a bit slow without newcomers," Mabel responded cheerfully.

Neither the mayor nor Tahini appeared to be as optimistic as Mabel.

As if on cue, the tinkling of the bell dangling from the shop's front door signaled the arrival of a new customer, and indeed it was a visitor, not one of the locals.

A tall, slender woman, dressed in black, silky bicycle gear, stepped into the shop, and with a long, slow stride, she moved toward the intake counter. Not even those with supernatural senses could hear her footsteps fall, she moved with such stealth and finesse. Her black hair was drawn back in a tight ponytail, accentuating the shape of her skull and in stark contrast to her nearly white skin. Her eyebrows were dark, thick, and perfectly shaped. A bit of pink sunburn across the bridge of her nose and a hint of red lip gloss were the only colors the woman bore.

Mabel scurried back to the counter to take the new arrival's order.

"What will you have, dear?"

"Hmmm," the woman purred, "what do you have with lots of milk?"

"We have latte or café au lait. Are you a sipper or a dipper?"

The woman's mouth curved into a small smile and replied, "I am more of a lapper."

"In that case, I would say our house special café au lait," Mabel suggested, and the woman nodded in agreement.

"I will take that to go," she said.

The bell tinkled again, and two young men, who appeared to be identical twins, walked in, jabbing each other in the pecs as they recklessly moved toward the counter.

Tahini's nostrils flared as a bitter, musky odor filled her nose and coated the back of her tongue, nearly triggering her gag reflex and causing the hairs on her arms to stand on end. The odor felt like a bristle brush rubbing over her skin.

"Siobhan, what is it?" the mayor asked.

"Shush! Don't call me that when strangers are around!" Teeny snapped in a harsh whisper she knew was rude and out of character, but she couldn't help herself, not with the sense of foreboding and danger suddenly filling her. She added more quietly, "Wait until they leave."

Mabel finished the preparation of her new customer's beverage, carefully snapped on the plastic lid, and slid the cup into a corrugated sleeve with the words "Broastful Brew" printed in a swirly script, similar to the steam that surrounded Tahini's head. Stepping around the two young men with a look of disgust, the slender woman left with the same quiet stealth as she entered, only the gentle ringing of the dangling bell noting her departure.

While Tahini found it odd to have so many newcomers in what was normally a quiet place, Mabel hopped around with a grin, obviously ecstatic that they'd chosen her little shop for their morning libations. The two strangers now in front of her requested cups of milk. She obliged them merrily. The jabbing brothers grabbed their cups, poking straws in the lids nearly simultaneously, paid Mabel, and exited the Broastful Brew.

Madame Tahini's shoulders gave a definitive shiver as she took a deep breath, her first one in several minutes. "Those two smell . . .

feral. That's the only way I can describe it. I don't like it. I hope they are only passing through, Barbie."

Barbie patted her friend's tiny hand. "Me, too, if they make you react like that. Maybe I should let Sheriff Kasun know to keep a watch out for them? They look goofy enough to be trouble."

Before Tahini could reply, Mabel bounced back to their table and inquired, "What do you think? I think that woman was fascinating. Have you ever seen skin so pale or hair so black? She walked like a cat. Did you see her eyes? Like emeralds, they're so green. Did you hear her voice? Like a purring sound was behind every word. Those boys, on the other hand, were a little feisty, but you know how kids are these days. Between Miss Café au Lait and the Hardy Boys, I'll probably have to stock up on more milk if they become regulars."

Barbie sat up straight and simply said, "Let's hope that's not necessary."

The two friends thanked Mabel and quickly gathered their belongings before exiting the coffee shop. Bending over at nearly a ninety-degree angle, Mayor Barbie hugged her little friend.

"I hope the day improves," she said as she straightened up.

"You and me both," Tahini replied as she grimaced at the awful odor still in her nose. "So far, the morning has literally left a bad taste in my mouth. But I'm sure there's a potion to take care of it, and I'm bound to find it. Good day, my friend."

Tahini started to turn, but Barbie placed a hand on her shoulder. "Remember to change the password."

"Oh, yes! It is time. Thank you for the reminder!"

The mayor smiled and shook her head before crossing Stuart Street, named after her ancestors, and headed toward City Hall, which sat on the north end of the town square. She frequently had to remind Teeny about her one duty for the town—updating and tracking the password for the residents' section of the Havenwood Falls website.

Unable to shake the ominous, odiferous sense that attacked her at Broastful Brew, Tahini crossed Eighth Street and strode at a brisk pace through Town Square Park, turning right and heading south, her hands fisted in her skirt pockets as she tried to quell their trembles. Still, another shiver racked her shoulders. Without pausing, she took a deep breath of fresh mountain air and raised her chin to catch the rays of the morning sunlight, needing what warmth they still provided on this late September day to calm her. Winter paid little attention to the calendar in these mountains, but the chill she felt through her body didn't come from the weather. *It must be those strangers. There's something not right, I just know it.*

On this brilliant fall morning, the sun beamed down on the fountain at the center of the square, causing it to sparkle with an uncanny glitter as the gold flakes in the bowl's paint caught the eastern light. The Stuarts had donated the flakes back in the town's beginnings during the gold mining days.

Tahini barely noticed the sparkles, though, as she moved as fast as her legs could carry her toward her own shop on the south side of the square—Madame Tahini's Potions, Lotions, Palm Readings, and Other Extra-Sensory Services. As she approached the curb to cross Main Street, she barely glanced both ways as her gaze slid across the buildings in front of her, from Simple Treasures Pawn Shop on the east end to The Haven Saloon on the west. Her own shop, Callie's Consignments, Coffee Haven, and Shelf Indulgence were sandwiched in between. Once she crossed the street in front of Coffee Haven, she inhaled the aroma of more coffee beans, which helped to relieve the olfactory memory of the feral boys at the other shop, at least for a few seconds.

By the time she hurried past Callie's and faced the door of her own shop, the odor had already returned, renewing Tahini's determination to find a potion or elixir that would remove that awful aroma forever. Her shop's door was made of heavy, roughly hewn boards with medieval silver hinges and handle. A very faint, long-ago carved etching of some otherworldly planetary alignment decorated the door. The design was barely visible in broad daylight, but the shadows cast in the morning and twilight hours could catch some of the distinctive motifs. A peephole door was set approximately four feet from the ground and could only be opened from the inside. A large, silver knocker shaped like a dragon's head hung above the peephole door.

Tahini removed a large black skeleton key from her skirt pocket, turned it in the lock, and pulled the heavy wooden door open. Once inside, she abruptly did an about-face, closed the door, and quickly slid the lock to its closed position. She gave a heavy sigh of relief as she turned back around to face her familiar, comfortable surroundings.

She stood in a small, dark foyer lined with ornate candle sconces and tapestries from all corners of the world. A clawed-foot, half-round table sat against the left-hand wall of the foyer, draped in a beaded shawl with a bowl of potpourri and an oversized candle in the center. Tahini replaced the key in her pocket and removed a box of matches, her fingers still quivering from her encounter as she slid the box open. She pulled a single match from the sleeve and struck it across the ignition side of the box. The match flew to life, and Tahini lit the table candle, illuminating the foyer.

She turned right and entered her "salon" through the hanging beads of its entryway. Teeny may have been tiny, but nothing about her décor, other than the low placement of the peephole, gave hint of it. The salon was lined on two sides of the room with built-in, floor-to-ceiling redwood bookcases, studded with dozens of large tomes, covered in various colors of leather and embossed with gold lettering. Some were kept shut with heavy locks, while others abounded with strands of colored ribbons as markers.

An enormous, overstuffed chair sat behind a round table draped similarly to the foyer table and stationed in the center of the room. The chair faced the salon window, which was inscribed in a Eurasian styled writing with her shop's name. The stereotypical glass globe perched in the middle of the table, although the globe itself was not exactly typical. A swirling mass of light and color remained in constant motion inside the glass orb. There were no electrical connections or batteries that caused these phenomena. Its incandescence and perpetual animation came from some other unexplainable source.

Teeny immediately went on the search for a potion, wheeling the librarian's ladder from the corner of the room to position it in front of the tallest shelf. Climbing to the fourth rung, she reached over to the volume covered in green leather and pulled it down from the shelf. As she stepped back off the ladder, the book slipped out of her arms and fell to the floor, opening flat to pages 110 and 111. The miniature medium bent over the book, examining the page carefully —a recipe for sorrel tea, guaranteed to remove noxious odors and toxins that may have infected the area.

"Thank you, Goddess." Tahini nodded to the spirits above, before pulling a maroon ribbon from the bottomless pocket of her skirt, which she placed between the pages. She carefully picked up the book and carried it out of her salon, nudging one of two tufted stools out of her way.

Tahini made her way to the kitchen in the back of her shop. She regarded her kitchen as her laboratory, because it appeared more like a mad scientist's workstation than that of a homey room designed to concoct comforting foods for the soul. She placed the book on the butcher block–style table and re-read the recipe, memorizing the ingredients required to brew the healing elixir.

> Wood Sorrel – two handfuls
> Goldenrod – one gram
> Charmed Spring Water – teapot full
> Spearmint leaf (optional)

Teeny took her favorite teapot, an intricately painted piece of pottery, from the breakfront cupboard and shoved it into one of her skirt pockets. She knew exactly where to gather the wood sorrel and goldenrod, still plentiful this time of year near the falls. There was ample spearmint growing in her backyard.

The little woman grabbed a long silk scarf off the coat hooks next to the back door and wrapped it around her head as she headed out the rear of the shop.

The sun spattered beams of light across a seemingly unkempt garden of varying herbs and flowers. Teeny crossed each of the stepping stones that led out to the water pump in the corner of the garden, where she filled her water bottle that she kept in her pocket, of course.

Swinging the wooden gate open, Tahini turned right down Memory Lane. She chuckled at the nomenclature for the narrow street, so dubbed by her fifth mother when it had just been a dirt path leading east to the big park. The memory spell of Havenwood Falls was originally formed behind the doors of the shop she had just left.

She passed the rears of several shops before coming to the end of the block where there was a parking lot behind The Haven Saloon, which also included a bicycle rack for the more athletic visitors to the town square district. Brent Hayes, saloon owner and bartender, leaned against the bike rack, toking on a joint, and waved as Tahini passed by.

"Good morning, Brent," Tahini greeted him. From the back of Brent's bar, one could look straight down Eighth Street and view the ski slopes at the end of the road. On a normal day, Teeny would have tossed a few clever words at "Bent Brent," such as "Can't wait 'til high noon?" to tease him about his early start. But this was no normal day, and she continued on her mission, intent on removing the stubborn odor.

Tahini considered shimmering to the falls, but chose the walk instead. This earthly realm was a kaleidoscope of sensations for Tahini, one in which she could smell sounds, hear colors, and touch and taste every scent. She enjoyed the cacophony of this world and wanted to make the most of the season before winter snows descended.

Tahini turned right down Eighth Street, her gaze sweeping the area for any signs of those stinky boys while her legs carried her as quickly as they could past Backwoods Sport & Ski, the Herbal Shoppe, and the rest of the town square business district. She rounded the corner onto Stuart Street and followed her regular path all the way down, past Cook's Corner park and the new library, to where the street ended at Blackstone Road. She skirted the two cemeteries—one for humans and one for not-so-humans—crossed the road, and came to one of the many trail heads in Havenwood Falls. A large decaying tree stump, with twisted and gnarled roots, guarded the trail entrance. Teeny took a seat to rest on its top, covered with felt-like moss, and pulled out her water bottle to take a sip.

As she sat rehydrating herself, a small moth-like insect began to buzz incessantly around Teeny's ear, nagging her emphatically.

"Just a moment, Silly Annie," she said and looked around to make sure there was no one watching.

Suddenly, Tahini's long, dark auburn hair began to turn solid white, starting from the ends and moving toward the roots. Her hair became totally white, her skin paled, and her entire being shone with a white so bright, one could practically see the prismatic colors that made it up. Thousands of small, effervescent bubbles began to rise from her skin and hair, and with a fizzle and a pop, Tahini seemed to have evaporated into thin air.

In truth, she'd only taken her true form.

"So what's the buzz, Silly Annie?" Tahini, who was by normal standards a very small woman, now stood only about five inches tall. Her body, totally entrenched in pure light and reflecting all visible color, like the fresh winter snows of the Rockies, teased the moth-sized creature at her side.

"First off, it's Cyllene," she said, adding, "pronounced see-lee-nee."

"Yeah, whatever, Silly Annie."

"Secondly, Siobhan, you nearly sat on me! My years are numbered as they are," the irritating creature yammered. Cyllene was an dryad, the soul of the tree Tahini had sat on, which had been felled by lightning years ago and was now slowly, laboriously decaying.

"I'm truly sorry, Silly Annie. I've just been a little distracted this morning. Are you okay? I'm okay." Tahini half-heartedly apologized. "Anything else? You were certainly making a nuisance of yourself, buzzing and bickering around my head, when all I needed was a cool drink of water. You know I can't discern a word you're saying when I'm in human form. So, again I ask you, what's the buzz?"

"My yes, there's something else! I wanted to warn you, if you are going up to the falls." Cyllene circled the stump and flew up to the top of the neighboring spruce, eyeing the entire landscape in her view. She returned to the stump.

"There's a black panther in the forest," she continued. "It's stealthy and fast, and I am sure it is viciously hungry for something! You must be extremely cautious, especially since you are walking, gods forbid. If you're going to the falls, why don't you just shimmer?"

"A black panther?" Tahini avoided the shimmer question. "Don't be silly, Silly Annie. There are no black panthers in this part of the world. Not even shifters."

Yet, Siobhan had an ominous feeling that this tale of Cyllene's rang all too true, and it had something to do with this morning's visitors at the Broastful Brew.

CHAPTER 2

AND A TROLL MAKES SEVEN

"*I* know there are no panthers here!" Cyllene exclaimed in answer. "I've only lived here for hundreds of years! But I'm telling you, it was a black panther, or maybe a jaguar, but completely, totally, awesomely black, nonetheless. It's dangerous, and it's on a mission."

The dryad appeared as a calamity of color, like a beautifully tattooed lady. Although her colors had begun to fade since her tree had fallen, they were still vibrant in the Colorado sunshine of autumn. Her wings were like those of a Madagascan sunset moth—large and billowy, and embellished with intricate, swirly veins of silver. She had long, flowing tails, nearly three times the size of her body, in an otherworldly, iridescent bluish-green. Both the forewings and hindwings were adorned with a circle of rainbow colors, emanating from violet at the center to red on the edges, representing all the hues that made up Cyllene's pallor.

Cyllene was now approximately three centimeters shorter than her long-time faerie friend, whom she knew as Siobhan. Her breadth more than made up for the difference in their height. The two together seemed an extraordinary contrast to one another, similar to Tahini and the Mayor. However, in her true form, Tahini was the reflection of all the shades of the universe combined that made up the individual skin tones of Cyllene. The two were, in an abstract way, the mirror image of one another.

Cyllene flapped her wings and began to fly around, taking to a flight pattern around and up and down the old stump's twisted roots, both fear and excitement on display in her luminescence and gyrations. Before her colors had begun to fade, it was easier to differentiate her emotions. Fear showed almost completely red, with dark maroon tones and shades of ghoulish grey. Her excitement had emitted as radiant tones of blue, yellow, emerald, and magenta, all of which pulsated to a beat that matched her level of enthusiasm. Now the colors swirled together, no longer as intense and distinctive as they'd once been.

For Tahini, this long goodbye was a loving and sad process to witness. She knew this dear nymph still had at least a hundred years or so to go, but time was micro and macro cosmic, and the years were only defined by humans in accordance their perception of their very tiny universe. That small thought made Teeny giggle to herself, but she regained her composure when she realized she needed to pay more attention to Silly Annie.

"Only one panther?" Siobhan finally asked.

"I certainly hope so. Isn't one enough?" Cyllene began to flitter nervously again. Tahini knew how her friend didn't like cats of any kind. They had a habit of batting at her.

Siobhan gave a bit of a shiver herself, since this morning's visitors had already set off her internal alarms with that uncanny and persistent odor. Even in her true form, it still offended her.

Cyllene alit on the stump next to her friend, evidently distraught, thinking Siobhan was not taking her as seriously as the situation called for.

Siobhan recognized her friend's angst and shared the story of the strangers in the coffee shop and the overwhelming odor of doom that incensed her. The two females determined they should go to the falls together. They also determined that Siobhan McFeeny was in no way *walking* to the falls, come hell or high water. No pun intended. For that matter, Cyllene suggested they find their friends—the four pixie sisters and Gruff the troll. Admittedly, they were all on the small side—what some might call little folk—but there was safety in numbers, and seven was always a lucky number.

"You go find the pixies," Siobhan said. "I need them to pick some goldenrod for me near Peacock Lake, so meet me there. I am sure I will find Gruff near Small's Falls."

Siobhan unfurled her wings—plumed, feathery, thin, and as blindingly white as the rest of her being. She had four thin wings buttressing each scapula—three forewings and a single hindwing on each side. Unlike Cyllene, who could only boast one upper wing and one lower wing on each side. However, Cyllene had the unusual and alluring flowing tails, whereas Siobhan's structure was built for speed. Such is the difference between the tasks of a nymph and those of a spring faerie.

The two lithe creatures took flight in a graceful flutter, heading north toward the great Havenwood Falls. Siobhan's form was the ultimate aerodynamic structure, and once her wings took lift and she picked up speed, they pulled back close to her body, and she shot through the air like a bullet. Cyllene, on the other hand, was built for beauty, music, and dance. Her large wings allowed her to practically float on a puff of wind. She was delicate and had to be careful, especially now in her weakened state, to not get stripped by an unnoticed thorn or caught in a spider's web. Siobhan took care not to fly too fast, in order to keep Cyllene in her line of vision.

One hundred meters before reaching the stupendous Havenwood Falls, Siobhan took a sharp left west. Cyllene continued on to seek out the pixies.

Siobhan came to a small, teal-colored lake, fed by a smaller set of three falls—the triplets. The lake spanned no more than a couple of hundred yards, formed partially by erosion from the trio of falls as well as by a small meteorite that had slammed into the base of the falls centuries ago. The spot was aptly named Small's Falls, not because of its size in comparison to the thunderous great falls, but because it was discovered by the intrepid prospector Rutherford Small.

Rutherford had been searching for the legendary great and mystical falls, but before he reached them, he came upon this lake and the triple falls that poured into it. Unfortunately for Rutherford, he never quite made it to the bigger falls. Rutherford did not know that the water was charmed—or cursed, depending on your perspective—and he refreshed himself by bathing in the lake and drinking from the falling water.

Peacock Lake at the bottom of Small's Falls offered many mystical powers, some harmful and some beneficial, but alas, none of the latter for humans. Instead, for these mere mortals, the lake only offered the evidence of their mortality, and poor Rutherford Small passed away, blissful as he sunned himself on the rocks and drifted into infinite sleep while listening to ethereal voices sing a lullaby.

Siobhan landed on the large boulder at the top of the center falls. A fizzling sound emanated from her tiny form, and as the sound grew louder, bubbles began to rise from her skin as she effervesced. The bubbles grew bigger and more colorful, as did Siobhan. Her solid white hair began to turn to auburn from the roots to the end, her skin took the human tone of a peachy caramel, and Teeny Weeny Tahini again stood at four feet five inches with a massive popping sound.

Teeny nimbly crossed the smaller rocks across the falls until she reached the mossy edge and leapt onto the padded grounds at the base of an enormous spruce. During the summer and fall, Teeny preferred to use her human form to navigate this peaceful territory. She enjoyed the smell of the soft texture of the moss and the prickly fragrance that tickled her nose when she touched the pine needles. The rich green shades of this sylvan place rang chords of low, soft tones in her ears.

Had it been winter, she would have remained as Siobhan the fae. Small's Falls would have been a frozen cavern of icy stalactites and monstrous frozen stalagmites. With the teal lake completely iced over and covered with powdered snow, she would have flitted from one icicle to the next, never noticed as she blended so perfectly with that wintry landscape.

On the eastern side of the spruce, Teeny sat down and pulled her teapot, the water bottle, and several vivid ribbons from her pockets. All of Teeny's ribbons were gifts from the pixie sisters, as collecting colored ribbons was one of their favorite hobbies. She began to gather the wood sorrel that grew plentifully on this side of the tree.

She then leaned over the southernmost triplet of the falls and holding the teapot by its handle, allowed the cool, falling water to easily fill it. Once the teapot was completely full, she poured the liquid springs into her water bottle and sealed it tight, wrapping an aqua hued ribbon around the neck for extra measure—or just for fun.

Cyllene returned, humming her familiar drone. Teeny could distinguish the excitement this time and told Cyllene she would follow her. The nymph fluttered off to the western edge of the lake, as Teeny walked nimbly around the edge of the still, peacock-colored waters.

Cyllene led her to a small step below the lake, where there was a wonderfully abundant patch of the yellowweed that Teeny required, along with the four sisters. The pixies had already begun collecting bunches of the goldenrod, although they lost most of it every time they broke into a wrestling match, which was often. Cyllene danced in the air as Teeny plucked a few dozen stems of the rods herself and wrapped them in a tangerine-toned ribbon.

"I gave you that ribbon!" shouted Enya, one of the pixies, with glee, proud to have her gift be of use.

Not quite sure how many reeds would constitute a gram, Teeny continued to pluck a few more stems when an ear-piercing howl caused lightning bolts to cross Teeny's vision.

The pain of that echoing screech ripped right through her, making her gasp.

"Stay close," she told the sprites before she set out to search for the injured party screeching that hurtful sound, which was now becoming a distressing moan.

She followed the lightning bolts that darted toward the north of the lake and through a copse of pines, Cyllene and the pixies close behind. In the rugged sagebrush, a snowy owl lay with one wing splayed awkwardly and unnaturally away from its body. Her heart wrenched at the sight, not only because she had a natural affinity to heal the harmed, but because snowy owls in particular held a special place in her heart. This one reminded her of her Aunt Abigail, a snow-white owl-shifter, but alas, she and her uncle were still on the other side of the great pond.

"Oh my, you dear thing. What happened to you?" Teeny spoke soothingly as she pulled her scarf from her head and swaddled the supine bird, being careful not to move too quickly and cause it any more pain.

The owl's large, enigmatic eyes took in the sight of Teeny, Cyllene, and their friends, and made a barely noticeable nod of thanks. The avian obviously could not have mustered more movement without experiencing excruciating pain.

"Cyllene, you and the girls go up to the cabin. I'm going to shimmer this poor child there."

With that, Cyllene took flight toward the open sky and disappeared, while the pixies skittered, leapt, and pirouetted toward the cabin.

Teeny checked her pockets to make sure she had all she had come for, then removed an olive green ribbon from her left pocket and carefully secured the swaddling scarf around the bird. She lifted the creature, who was amazingly light for its size, and held it gently in her arms.

Before she could begin her shimmer, a gravelly voice called out to her from one of the nearby caves. She turned to find Gruff waving madly, beckoning her to come.

"I'll be right back, little owl. I need to speak to the troll." She gently placed the bird back on the ground then walked over to the cave, where Gruff anxiously paced. Gruff stood no taller than Teeny, but quite a bit stouter. His skin was mottled gray, but he had deep, dark brown eyes that pierced one's soul.

"What's up, Gruff? Why are you in such a snit? I mean, more than your normal self."

"Look what someone left in my cave!" he barked, jabbing his gnarly finger at the back wall of the grotto.

Teeny's hand flew to her mouth to stifle a gasp as she spied the form. A mummified body, loosely wrapped in a black shroud, had invaded Gruff's hole in the mountain!

"Oh my, that's wretched!" A shiver wracked Teeny's whole body, and it took her a moment to regain her composure. "Gruff, meet me at my cabin. You can stay there for the night. I found an injured owl, and I need to take care of him, but I'll call Sheriff Kasun when we get there and have him retrieve the . . . the body."

With another shudder, Teeny turned and hurried as far away from the corpse as she could, returning to the ailing owl. She cautiously picked him up and held him gently to her chest. She closed her eyes, and the air surrounding them grew perfectly still. Silver sparkles seemed to rain down from nowhere, as Teeny and her patient became translucent, rippled, and then vanished completely, leaving only a few remnant sparkles behind.

Several hundred feet from where Teeny had found the snowy owl, silvery flakes of light sprinkled down upon the front porch of a small A-frame cabin nestled in a stand of bristlecone pines. A simple wooden structure, with a single, triangular-shaped door just tall enough to clear Teeny's head and a small shuttered window above, the cabin was adorned at the front and back peaks with ornately carved wooden scrolls. A rippling of the air began to appear as Teeny arrived from nothing to translucent to her opaqueness, still holding the injured animal close to her breast to protect it from any shimmer effects that may have occurred.

Opening the cabin door with a pearly key she withdrew from her right pocket, Teeny bent her head down just a bit for extra clearance and entered the compact building. She left the door open for Cyllene and the crew's arrival, moved toward a rustic bench padded with a tapestried cushion, and gently placed the owl upon it.

Teeny shimmied up the knotted rope that hung from the loft to open the window shutters—one in front and one in back—letting the pine-sifted sunlight into the cabin. As she descended from the loft, Cyllene flew through the cabin's entry and took a landing place on the washstand at the back of the solitary room that made up the living space of the cabin. Unlike Teeny's salon home in town, the cabin was furnished sparsely, designed for refuge and recluse. It offered austere harmony without all the external stimuli.

"Cyllene, could you light the candles for me, please?" Teeny requested.

Any request that Cyllene received from Teeny was like manna from heaven to her. Candle lighting was a special talent of Cyllene's, and she was always pleased to perform this task. Cyllene fluttered over to the first sconce by the open door, circled around the candle three times, then spiraled above it, letting her swallow tails spin into a helix. *Poof!* The candle was lit. She fluttered around the room to each sconce, twirling and whirling until all the candles in the room had her flamed glory.

The pixies danced into the great room, happily waving their stems of goldenrod and covering the floor with the yellow pollen that sprayed from the flowers.

"Oh look, we've made a golden carpet for Siobhan!" announced Aeiri.

Ushka began to swirl around and dance through the canary-colored dust, making intricate designs.

With the cabin awakened by the firelight of the sconces, Teeny closed the front door and went over to the bench that would now serve as the triage gurney for the harmed owl. The owl's eyes were bigger than ever, but there was no response to the light. Its pupils were fixed and dilated, and its feathery limbs shook as if there was a small quake underfoot. Teeny feared for the unfortunate fouled fowl.

Cyllene started her incessant murmuring, so Teeny fetched a tin funnel from the cabinet and placed it on a makeshift clamp on the table across the room from the padded bench. Cyllene, with many years of practice at using the funnel-clamp contraption, took her place by the narrow end.

"What's that black thing sticking out of its back?" The question shouted out of the large end of the funnel, as Cyllene's voice became more than an insect's buzz.

Teeny gently turned the fowl creature over to its left side and saw a large black splinter lodged in its scapula. "I didn't see that! I was so concerned with moving him."

She pinched her small fingers to remove the protrusion from the bird's back, but no sooner than she touched it, she soared clear across the room and smashed into the table where Cyllene had been speaking through her home-styled megaphone.

Teeny lay face up in the center of the cabin in a daze. All of her pockets spilt onto the floor in an array of chromatic ribbons, keys, her teapot, water bottle, wood sorrel, goldenrod, and a sprig of spearmint.

CHAPTER 3

POTIONS AND NOTIONS

"*S*iobhan! Are you okay?" came the worried voice of Cyllene through the funnel.

There was no response.

Except a loud knock at the door.

Gruff entered the cabin without waiting for an invitation. He found Teeny lying on the floor, seemingly unconscious, and rushed to her side.

Cyllene, although diminishing with her felled tree soul, now became a deep maroon with worry, and the silver lines shone brightly through her skin and wings. She eyed the water bottle lying close to Teeny and flitted to it. In a ruffling of wings and tail, Cyllene whipped up a small whirlwind under the water bottle, and the swirling air, expertly maneuvered, caught under the cylindrical vessel. The bottle rolled toward Teeny's head as she lay limply on the hardwood floor of the cabin.

Gruff picked up the bottle and held it to Tahini's lips, urging the unconscious faerie to drink.

Cyllene managed to pick up a small leaf of spearmint that had fallen out of Teeny's pocket, and she placed it beneath her friend's nostril. Then she whirled up, causing another twister that forced the spearmint into Teeny's nasal cavity.

Teeny's eyes flickered and fluttered, and she blinked up at Gruff, dazed and disoriented.

Cyllene flew back to the makeshift microphone and ordered, "Siobhan! Drink from the water bottle! It's filled with Peacock Lake water, remember?"

Teeny followed Cyllene's order. Although weak and barely able, she took a small sip from the bottle Gruff held before her. In what seemed like a human's lifetime to Cyllene, but was only a matter of minutes, Teeny recovered and finally sat up. She shook her henna-tinted locks, and her long dark lashes fluttered rapidly.

"Well, that was quite a hit. Bent Brent doesn't know what he's missing," came the first words out of Teeny's mouth.

Cyllene and the others laughed, relief flooding the room.

As Teeny continued to recuperate, she rolled over to her left side and eyed her porcelain teapot, now cracked after centuries of use, a sprawl of sorrel, and a spray of goldenrod which left its yellow dusting across the floor.

She then rolled over on her right side, movement being just a bit hindered by her weakness, and found her keys, both the ebony and the pearl, scattered by her side, along with her two bundles of sorrel, safely tied with the lavender and turquoise ribbons. Miscellaneous multicolored ribbons were strewn at her feet. A great sigh of relief breathed from her.

The pixies picked up the strewn ribbons and began to wave them above their heads as they danced in a circle around Tahini, celebrating her recovery.

As Teeny regained her strength, she realized the owl had been completely silent. She was not oblivious to Cyllene and Gruff saving her life, but there were more urgent issues at hand. Teeny stood up on wobbly legs, and went back to the bird that was now exposing its backside.

"This thing must be made of iron," Tahini said upon closer inspection of the thorn or splinter. "No wonder it hit me so hard."

Iron was Tahini's allergy, her weakness, her total vulnerability. It explained the blast that threw her across the room and her inability to regain her strength quickly.

Tahini continued, "I need to be able to speak with this woodland creature. Perhaps it will be able to tell me what happened to him, and maybe he even knows who put a dead body in Gruff's cave."

"Dead body?" screeched Tierri, one of the pixies, dancing nervously now.

"Right by my bed!" Gruff huffed.

"We'll worry about that in a moment," Teeny promised. "First, we need to save this owl. Girls, I need a couple of twigs, very small and flat. Do you think you can find those for me?"

The pixies all nodded in unison and danced past Gruff and out of the cabin to gather Teeny's requested items, and Cyllene floated out the loft window to supervise the mischievous little faeries.

Moments later, twigs of every shape and size dropped down from the loft and fell onto the pollen-coated floor.

Cyllene furiously fluttered in and out of the cabin's window, as she instructed the pixies on which twigs to choose. She had to keep a close eye on them, since she was an dryad borne of trees. The twigs had to be fallen branches, those that would not survive without their Mother Tree, and could have no nuts or seedlings attached to them. Nevertheless, Cyllene's keen eyesight enabled her to ensure the pixies selected an immense number of twigs and sticks from which Siobhan could choose.

Tahini scanned the mass array of tinder scattered on the floor and chose two fairly flat sprigs of nearly even lengths. She pulled a cocoa-colored ribbon from her pocket, set the end of it between her teeth, and split the ribbon in half, straight down the middle through its full length, leaving her with two thinner threads.

"I gave her that one, and look, she's doubled my gift!" Tierri said delightedly.

Teeny wrapped the top of the shoots to fashion a primitive pair of tweezers, with enough twine between to give them proper leverage.

"I hope I have enough strength to remove it with this," Teeny said, praying the owl would get the hint that they were here to help.

Still weakened by the kryptonite-like blow, Teeny wobbled over to the large chest at the end of the cushioned bench. Fumbling through various articles stored in the chest, with a clattering of metal and glass and a rustling of wool and cotton, Teeny pulled out a bell jar and stand.

Placing them near the owl's head, she cautiously rolled the fowl to its left side to get a better angle at the splinter protruding from its body. A series of clicks, snaps, trills, and hoots emerged from Teeny's throat as she soothed the white bird, carefully maneuvering the primitive tongs to release the offensive object from its shoulder blade. Despite a few twists and tugs at the thorn and some throaty moans from the bird, Teeny was unable to withdraw the barb.

"I do it, Siobhan." Gruff uncharacteristically offered his assistance. A simple tug of the tweezers from the stout but strong troll, and the black claw-like thing came loose from the owl's flesh and fell on the floor.

Teeny quickly slammed the bell jar on top of it.

For a few seconds, the blackened hook glowed a blood red color, then faded back to its original darkness. The smell of the thing reminded her of the pungent, awful odor during this morning's coffee. She tried not to gag. Now more than ever she had to brew her sorrel tea.

Gathering sticks and logs from a basket, Teeny built a fire in her pot-bellied stove, which Cyllene happily lit. The stove began to glow as the room warmed. Teeny filled her teapot with the remaining falls water and placed it on top of the stove. While it heated, she measured ingredients with her apothecary scale and added them to the pot, including a couple of spearmint leaves to cover the lemony scent of the sorrel. Lemon was another of her allergies, and the scent alone made her lips pucker. As the tea brewed, the room began to take on a minty aroma, and even before Teeny had a chance to sip the potion, she already felt the heavy gloom of the morning begin to lift.

Meanwhile, Cyllene kept a worried watch over their avian guest lying limply on the bench and not seeming to recuperate very quickly. Cyllene's complexion grew pale as the cabin drew darker, the sun making its dreamy descent behind the mountain.

After retrieving a couple of teacups, an eyedropper, and a small sieve from the chest, Teeny poured the steaming liquid into each cup, moving the sieve each time to catch the loose leaves and blossoms. She took a couple of sips from one cup, allowing the steamy fumes to engulf her senses. For the first time since this morning, Teeny began to feel like her normal self.

She then used the eyedropper to remove some of the broth from the second cup and went over to the owl. She gently prodded the bird's beak open with the end of the syringe, slipping a few drops of the healing brew into its throat. Teeny whispered comforting hoots and whistles into the owl's ears.

The owl ruffled a few feathers, and Cyllene brightened. The dryad flew back to the table and took her station at her tin microphone.

"I didn't know you could speak owl," she stated.

"Oh, yes, Bubo scandiacus have been in my family tree for centuries." Teeny giggled.

"What's so funny?"

"Owls. Trees. Get it? Owls in my family tree?"

"Oh, very cute."

Teeny applied a few more droplets to the wound on the owl's back and smiled as she witnessed the hole heal and close up. Using several silk scarves from the trunk, Teeny formed a nest around the bird, making a satiny fortress to protect it as it recovered.

"It's been a long day. It's time to rest. Thanks to all of you for your help."

The pixie sisters danced out of the cabin to head for home, and Teeny locked the front door behind them before she snuffed the candles out on the first floor. She shimmied up to the loft and tossed a few pillows and a blanket down to the troll.

"Gruff, you can set up a bed down there, next to the owl."

Cyllene, happily hovering over Teeny, watched as Teeny shuttered and locked the back window and went to the front one.

"You need some sleep, too, Silly Annie. I will see you in the morning."

Cyllene buzzed and whirred and then flew out the loft's opening and into the night, the moonbeams causing her wings to glow ever brighter. Teeny shuttered and locked the front window, grabbed a blanket from the loft chest, and nestled into her bed, utterly exhausted.

CHAPTER 4

NOXIOUS DEVOTIONS

On the far end of the canyon, secluded deep in the woods, Shayin Pisik stood at the window of her rented cabin. The reflection of her dark hair flowing over her shoulders, her pale skin, and her lithe body clad in black lace and silk had initially caught her attention, but now she gazed through the image, into the night outside. She saw perfectly into the darkness, though she was surrounded by trees that reached high into the sky, the feathery tops of the pines pointing toward the stars. One hand rested on her narrow waist, her fingers tapping a slow rhythm against her hip bone while the other hand moved her locket back and forth on its chain around her neck. Trying to ignore the faint ache at the tip of one of her fingers, she focused her thoughts elsewhere. If everything went as planned, she'd be reunited with her love in a week's time. Her stomach fluttered with giddiness at the thought of being in his arms again for the first time in decades.

Unfortunately, she'd had to rely on others to execute today's phase of the plan, and she'd yet to hear if all had gone well.

She turned from the darkness outside and padded over to the kitchen. She needed a warm glass of milk to calm her nerves. Just as she curled herself onto the leather sofa, glass in hand, her phone buzzed on the end table, indicating a text message.

Thing One: We lost him

Her hackles immediately rose, and a growl rumbled in Shay's chest.

Shay: WTF does that mean?

No answer came. She sprang to her feet and paced across the cabin, hating the feel of the wood floor on the pads of her soles. Just one more thing to annoy her. Finally, her phone rattled on the table again. She glanced down at it.

Thing One: We searched everywhere. He's gone.

Shay hissed loudly as she snatched her phone off the table. She tapped furiously at the screen, but her response wouldn't send. The icon at the top showed No Service. A string of profanities flew out of her mouth along with a spray of spittle. She heaved the phone at the log wall, where it smacked and dropped to the floor with the distinct sound of glass cracking.

"Just fabulous," she snarled as she stalked for the front door. She threw it open, embracing the cool night air, and strode out into the dark woods on a mission. She shed the thin fabric of her lingerie, called to her inner nature, and a moment later, she was gone.

A LARGE BLACK feline strode toward the front porch of the cabin in the woods, a red fox clamped in its jaws, blood dripping a path up the steps. The creature was much too large for a house cat and not one that belonged in this forest, or even in this part of the world. Of course, Havenwood Falls attracted all kinds, including special kinds of wildlife. The panther, for there was no denying it was a black panther, dropped its prize on the doormat of the cabin, gracefully turned, and disappeared into the darkness of night.

A while later, the panther returned, this time depositing a bloodied rabbit. And then again the feline came to the cabin, its powerful muscles undulating under its shiny black fur as it climbed the steps and gifted the occupant with a squirrel. This time when it disappeared, its black fur blending in with the blackness of the woods, it didn't return.

~

SHAY PICKED up her discarded lingerie and sauntered toward the cabin in a much better mood. She was glad she'd thought to rent her own place away from town and the others, where she could prowl the woods as she liked, in all her natural glory. She stopped at the door, in front of the mat, which was drenched in crimson and piled with fur. She grinned at the bounty before her, gathered the animal corpses, still warm and fresh, and went inside.

"Some things you just have to do for yourself," she muttered as she placed the animals on the kitchen counter.

She disappeared into the bedroom, but when she returned with arms full, she still remained naked as the day she was born. She paused in front of the window, admiring her reflection and its endless youth and beauty again, before crossing to the kitchen and depositing the items she'd collected from her luggage next to the corpses.

She set the iron bowl in the center of the counter and arranged the candles around it. With a flick of her fingers, flames flew up on the wicks. Next, she poured a line of salt that began to take the shape of a sigil in and around the candles. One by one, she added ingredients into the bowl—a mixture of herbs, along with a few strands from the lock of hair she kept in a glass jar and a white feather. She then picked up the squirrel, pierced her fingernail into its chest cavity, and extracted its heart. She squeezed the organ like a grape, the blood oozing over her hand and into the bowl. She repeated the process with the rabbit and the fox. Finally, she picked up the dagger and sliced across her palm, adding her own blood to the mixture.

She closed her eyes and chanted under her breath as she waved her hands over the bowl. In a few moments, a large flame burst from the vessel. Her lips spread into a wicked grin as she opened her eyes and grasped her locket, holding it over the flame. With a squeeze of her fingers, it sprang open.

She recited the words loud and clear:

> Heart of Darkness on this chain,
> Holder of answers, do proclaim!
> Your eye is sagacious, sharp, and shrewd,
> Tell me what you know is true!

A crimson mist rose from the locket and swirled above it, mixing in with the smoke from the flame below. A voice sang, a low tenor, from the shapeless fog.

> Greater Pisik, Lady Shayin
> Master of darkness that flows within
> You once yearned to be the fairest of all
> But that is no longer why you call.

Shay rolled her eyes at the mist. She'd moved on from that petty need eons ago. All that mattered now was rejoining with her one true love. "You know what I want."

The mist swirled in acknowledgement and answered:

> Here is the way to find your prey:
> In the woods nearby, with a fae.
> But be forewarned that what you seek
> Will be lost to you within the week.

Shay growled at the locket as she snapped it closed. "I asked for facts, not lame advice!"

But at least she now had an idea of where to finally capture that which had eluded her for so long. Soon, she would be rejoined with her love.

CHAPTER 5

HOOT AND HOLLER

*T*eeny awoke before dawn. She went to the steamer-style trunk and selected a pale pink frock splattered with hand-painted, sea-green butterflies. On closer inspection, one could see that they were not butterflies at all, but tiny clones of Cyllene. At first, Cyllene was not very happy modeling for the image, but the finished product delighted her. As with all of Teeny's clothing, large blossomy pockets were on each side of the dress.

Teeny bought all of her clothing at one place only: Dress Perfect, owned by her friend Nina. Nina's clothing designs were original with a very Havenwood Falls-ish style and function. Long ago, Tahini brought her a pattern idea for her skirts. She had sketched out for Nina a basic daisy design with petal-like layers and large pockets on each hip. The dressmaker took barely a day to turn the rough sketch into the finished skirt that became Tahini's trademark. Nina kept an eye out for unusual fabrics that appealed to Teeny's "nature" sense. Often, the two women would sit up late at night and hand-paint the motifs onto the skirts.

Recalling yesterday's events and the ill owl that was now her patient, Teeny was determined to equip her cabin with everything she could think of to help heal the bird. Of course, everything she needed was in her salon in town, and the best way to gather those articles would be to shimmer there, and so she did.

Tahini found that certain tasks were more expedient or less exhausting when she was in her human form. Shimmering took energy, from both time and space. She could get to one place from another in a wing's beat, but it affected the universe. She often observed that when she shimmered, the human world was also in the ripple, and it would take a blink or two before the humans caught up with her in time, or maybe it was vice versa. Every now and then, it was much longer than a few seconds, sometimes hours. It was akin to jet lag, in a way.

As Teeny paraphrased the experience, "There is glimmer in the shimmer, but a stipple in the ripple."

When she shimmered, however, she was able to take large objects with her. Effervescing was a totally different scenario. When she effervesced, Tahini became Siobhan, her Gaelic faerie-self. She could shoot to her target location, much like a .22 cartridge shot out of a Winchester rifle. Upon arrival, she could effect "personal service." As Siobhan the spring fae, her talents were of a magical nature. She could cast spells, make humans lose their memories or feeling in their limbs, or cause a variety of very unpleasant and uncomfortable syndromes. She had limited abilities among supernaturals, depending on the species. Some things were better left to the human side of her.

Rippling into the shop, Teeny first went to examine her library. On a bottom shelf was a thick book with a brown suede cover. The title read *Big Bold Beautiful Bird Encyclopedia of Bubo Scandiacus*. Teeny read the words over and over, simply because she liked the sound of how they rolled off the tongue, as she removed the book and placed it on the round table in the salon.

"I definitely need the HOHUM," she said aloud. She turned to select a red leather-bound book with a number of colored ribbons marking pages throughout. The title read *Handbook of Healing Unctions and Mixtures*. She placed this book atop the encyclopedia and gazed into the crystal ball still mysteriously ablaze in the center of the table.

In the middle of the sphere appeared a large, old alder with great branches and many limbs.

"Hmm . . . I didn't think I would need that, but okay," she replied to the globe.

She climbed the librarian's ladder to the top rung and removed a dust-covered album from the highest shelf. She brushed off the dust on the wooden cover of the scrapbook, which was emblazoned with a family crest.

"Love, Loyalty, Longevity" was the translation of the family motto "Amor Pietas Grandaevitas" inscribed on the banner. The shield pictured a large tree illustrating the four seasons, symbolizing longevity. It was surrounded by thorny rose bushes, symbolizing love. Atop the coat of arms, a snowy owl, Bubo scandiacus, with its wings spread out across the width of the crest, represented the family's protector, the overseer of the forest. The album was added to the family collection when her father's brother Seamus had married an owl-shifter. The beloved Abigail became as much of a family member as all the faerie kin.

She collected her tomes and went into the kitchen, where she gathered a cheesecloth bag, a pair of stork-shaped scissors, and her ever-handy Swiss army knife, all of which she dropped into her frock pocket. Then, for the first time since the new moon waxed crescent, Tahini went up the stairs of her shop apartment and pulled the rope that held the attic spring door in place.

The attic, unlike what most would expect, was not cluttered nor covered with cobwebs. It was immaculately organized and obviously had constant care. Teeny went to the far northwest corner, where she seldom had to roam, and found the expertly hand-crafted wooden box, made up of a variety of different woods, smooth and gleaming, with a latch that was made of silver and embedded with abalone. There was no keyhole for the box and no way of entry that any person could discern.

Teeny passed her hand in a smooth and gliding gesture in front of the latch, and the seemingly impenetrable lock snapped open. Inside, silk pouches of varied colors and sizes nestled in the bottom of the box, each little bag containing a portion of Teeny's faerie dust. She kept it locked up tight, because its potency attracted many of the wrong kind of folk. She herself only used it for emergencies. She didn't know what this new day would bring, but a body in a cave, a sick owl, and a hard hit of iron all in one day were enough to convince her that she couldn't be too prepared. So she selected a few different sized bags, stuffed a small one in her bra ("just in case"), and dropped the others in her deep pockets.

After running a Swiffer duster, which was far more efficient and less messy than a feather duster, over the furnishings stowed in the attic, Tahini descended the ladder and released the spring. The attic door snapped closed, and the rope recoiled into nothingness, like a retractable cord on a vacuum cleaner.

She exited her salon home as she had the day before, through the back door in the kitchen, and stepped into her overgrown garden. Using the stork scissors, she snipped large sprigs of lavender, bunches of rosemary, some chamomile, wintergreen, and a healthy handful of dill. She turned to face a lush aloe plant and releasing the sawblade of her Swiss army knife, sheared off a large branch of the succulent and immediately shoved it into the cheesecloth pouch, along with the rest of her herbs. She looked around to see if there was anyone watching, not that most anyone could see her diminutive personage in this overgrown garden, but when she shimmered, no one or thing could be trusted. Just before she instituted her ripple, she caught eye of a patch of catnip on the far side of the water pump, and she remembered Cyllene's warning of the panther.

"Just in case," Teeny muttered to herself, and she nabbed an entire plant right out of the ground.

Time wrinkled.

The sun was rising over the east side of the canyon town when Tahini's ruffled wave appeared at the trail head to Havenwood Falls and Cyllene's homestead.

"Silly Annie? Wake up!" she shouted into the deaf tree.

A glimpse of phosphorescence emerged from the barren trunk.

Cyllene stretched and yawned and bent her face up to the new light of the day. She was still here and so was her favored pine. And so was her next favored one, Siobhan.

"Let's go!" Tahini commanded. "There is much to do."

The small translucent rippling wave of air and time took Teeny back to the cabin.

Cyllene could have hitched a ride on that awesome surf, but shimmering made her seasick. The nymph preferred the more relaxing course of gliding on the wind's breeze and basking in the glory of the early morning light, so similar and so different from the lunar illumination of the preceding evening.

When Teeny arrived at the front door of the cabin and rippled back to herself, she looked up into the sky to see if Cyllene had caught up with her. She fumbled for the pearl key in her frock pocket, shifting the books in her arms to unlock the door. Another glance at the sky, and she spotted her friend gliding toward her.

She unlocked the cabin door and left it wide open for Cyllene as she stepped into the great room of the A-frame.

And she let loose a blood-curdling scream.

A large naked man was curled up in the middle of the floor, and Gruff was sitting in the corner, quivering in fear!

Teeny let out another scream and grappled for the Swiss Army knife in her deep pocket, but was only able to catch the nipping scissors.

Cyllene, hearing her friend's scream, increased her speed and flew into the cabin. Knowing the human man lying on the floor caused the commotion, she began to buzz fiercely around the intruder's head.

While Cyllene expertly annoyed the stranger, Teeny scanned the cabin and realized the owl was nowhere to be seen, and she had left the cabin locked up when she departed before daylight this morning. Did Gruff let him out? But she noted the impossibility of this enormous human fitting through her small cabin door, which was purposely built to be tall enough for her and nothing larger.

She pointed the stork scissors threateningly at the invader, shouting, "Who are you? Where's the owl? What do you want?"

At that moment, the pixies marched into the cabin, single-file.

"Is everyone okay? We heard screams," said Tierri.

"It was a screech," Aeiri corrected her sister.

"No, it was more like a holler," Enya disagreed.

"Wrong, it was a cry," Ushka added to the bickering group.

The stranger lifted his head, and thick locks of white hair with streaks of brown tumbled onto his muscular shoulders. His smooth skin, all of it, was a shiny, sun-kissed honey color. Teeny noted a gash on his back that appeared to be in the process of healing.

The man turned his face toward Tahini, and she looked deep into his amber eyes. Her own eyes grew larger with sudden recognition.

She cried out excitedly, "Mat? Mathieu?" She began to hop on one foot and then the other, dancing a jig around the room. "Oh my gods, Mathew, it's you! Mathew, it's you!"

Cyllene said, "Gods bless you," as it sounded to her as if Siobhan was sneezing.

"Aunt Siobhan?" a deep, calm voice gently replied from the human being on the floor. He pronounced Siobhan like "chiffon" and the "aunt" nearly rhymed.

"Aunt Siobhan?" Gruff questioned with a huff.

Teeny was still dancing around the great room, singing out, "Mat, Ma-tew, Mateus, Mateo, Mathew, Mat, Mat, Mat, it's really you!"

Cyllene, completely confused by the scene, took her position at the funnel and asked, "What in the name of Zeus is going on?"

"It's my nephew Mathew!" Tahini responded with a giggle, since nephew and Mathew sort of rhymed, like Aunt Siobhan sort of rhymed.

"Nephew? What nephew?" Gruff's questioning became more insistent.

"Well, not really my nephew. He's my cousin, but he's so much younger than me, by a few hundred years, that for all intents and purposes, I'm his aunt."

The handsome being modestly covered up his private parts with his large, man hands, and his mouth turned into a devastatingly gorgeous smile. He gleamed up at Teeny with his golden eyes.

"I found you! Or you found me, I should say? Father and Mother sent me here to look for you."

Teeny calmed herself down and went to the bench where the owl had left the many scarves that had formed its bed. She picked out the largest one and told Mathew to stand up. He obeyed, and she wrapped the scarf around his waist, rolling and folding the cloth, sarong style.

"Well, aren't we bashful?" commented Cyllene. Of course, the nymph wore no clothes, but her skin was so chromatic, one could barely tell she was bare.

Mat took a seat on the cushioned bench, and Teeny sat beside him. She wrapped her arms halfway around his chest and back, as that was all she could reach.

She explained to Cyllene that Mathew, Mat, was the son of her father's brother, Seamus McFeeny, who had married an owl-shifter, a wonderfully wise and thoughtful woman who apparently had a strong gene pool.

"Goodness to Gwyllion, what brings you here? I have not seen you since you were an owlet, like a hundred years ago." Tahini pressed her nephew for answers.

This meant she hadn't seen Mat since he reached maturity, and because he was male, that meant Mathew was the equivalent of twenty-one human years old. Owl-shifters could not shift until they were physically mature, and then could not shift at will until emotionally mature, which could be quite a few decades away still.

The owl's maturity day was a time for celebration, when the parents of the young adults introduced their children to the abilities of shifting and the duties they were to carry forward as the Knights of the Forest, protecting the vulnerable, both plant and animal alike.

"I'm going to make us some sassafras root tea, and you can tell me about everything," Teeny announced as she went to the kitchen-like portion of her cabin.

"I really don't know all the details," Mathew started as Teeny poured the tea. "Mother and Father seemed to be a bit secretive about it, like they were protecting me from some kind of danger. But we have been traveling for more than twenty years from Gwynf'l to Ireland to Canada, I guess trying to avoid or escape the danger they whispered about. The peril apparently had come very close when we were in Alberta. That's when Mother and Father thought I would be safer here with you, and they sent me to find you."

"You are safe, my dear Mat. But what happened to you in the woods?"

He scratched his jaw and squinted his eyes. "I was attacked, but I'm not sure by what. All I know is that as soon as I was struck, I flew off as fast and as far as I could go, but the wound didn't heal like it normally would. I made it as far as I could, following the pull I felt in my soul, before I couldn't move at all. I fell to the ground, like a stuffed bird. I don't even know how long I lay there until you found me."

Teeny's mood darkened at the word "attacked." She stood up and retrieved the bell jar that held the ominous thorn.

"This is what we found lodged in your back. I believe it's made of iron. That's why you weren't able to heal, having faerie blood and all. It's probably why you didn't shift at daylight, as well. I took a wild blow myself trying to remove it. Thank the gods and goddesses that Gruff was here to help."

Gruff smiled sheepishly, unaccustomed to compliments.

SOME IRON MUST HAVE LEAKED into Mat's blood, because he should have healed almost instantly, but he didn't. Teeny's HOHUM book provided her with the proper assortment of herbal remedies to enhance his recovery, along with her Aunt Siobhan tender loving care. Within a couple of days, spent catching each other up on life since the last time they saw each other, Mat was finally able to fly again.

Unlike the natural snowy owls (compared to the supernatural), Mat flew at night, after sunset brought on the shift. He went out that first night through the loft window to forage and rejuvenate himself, returning at dawn to the safety of Teeny Weeny's cabin. Teeny noticed that although Mat had regained his owl prowess, his human side still suffered. The beautiful honey buff that he bore had become ashen, and she'd found strands of his hair loitering around the great room.

"Now that you're up and about, it's time we get you out of this cramped cabin. It's made for teeny people, not grown men. I'll take you to my town home. It's a normal place, kinda," Siobhan said to him the next morning, although it was close to noon already. Mat was a late riser after being out a good part of the night. "I'll go now to prepare the town home for you. I need to bring so much with me, I can't take you, too, Mat. We might lose too much time in the ripple. We could even lose each other!"

"You'll come back for me then?" Mat asked.

His aunt sighed. "I wish I could, dear nephew, but shimmering takes too much out of me, and I'm still not quite back to normal after that iron hit. Tonight, Silly Annie will show you the way to my home. I'll leave the loft window open."

As a deity and a nymph of the forest, there long before the Old Families ever came to the box canyon that became Havenwood Falls, Cyllene had special privileges, including being able to retain her natural form in town rather than having to appear human. After all, she simply seemed to be a lunar moth and nothing more. Sometimes staying in her tree stump became intolerably lonely, so she went to town frequently to visit Teeny and other friends. She would have no problem leading Mat to town tonight.

Teeny gathered her books and other supplies she'd brought from the town home and dropped them into her bottomless pockets. Today she wore a skirt that was another of her and Nina's late-night efforts. It was made of muslin and painted with ivy vines, dark green leaves, and bright holly berries. Tahini had added a sprinkling of faerie dust to the fireflies they had painted throughout the design, making them appear to flash on and off as the sunlight caught them.

Shortly before dusk, Cyllene flew into the cabin window and settled on the table across from the overgrown creature and eyed him curiously.

As the sun began to set, Mat tossed his long locks and stretched his arms out to his side, preparing for the shift. Cyllene watched the mesmerizing transformation of Mat the Man to the Tiger of the Trees. His hair grew shorter, then turned to a feathery mass. The smooth skin of his outstretched arms became covered in down, and long, tiger-striped, primary covert feathers began to form, followed by the secondaries, his mantle, collar, and tail feathers. His barrel chest and ripped abs became proportionately smaller with his diminishing size, as his trunk seemed to disappear into a flurry of tail feathers, flank, tibia, tarsus, and clawed feet.

Cyllene now looked upon a magnificently handsome, winged creature that stood before her on strong talons.

"That was amazing!" Cyllene said. Now that the two were both of the woodland creature size, Mat could understand Cyllene's whirring muses.

"And invigorating. I see and hear everything so much better now," Mat responded as he turned his head practically 180 degrees to take in the humble surroundings. The two creatures had no difficulty in communicating with each other in their natural forms. "Let's go!"

Cyllene mumbled to herself, "Well, there's a familiar family trait."

The pair took flight out the loft window and into the night sky. Mat's keen eyesight made it easy to follow the butterfly moth as she floated over the treetops. His peripheral vision allowed him to take in the landscape of the canyon, the falls (both great and Small's), and his dinner hopping along the forest floor. Unable to witness him partake in his spoils, Cyllene remained high above, watching for that panther. She reported spying a few known shifters from town and steered Mat away from them, since he hadn't received the town's protective mark yet. Thankfully, there was no sign of the large cat. Perhaps it had already moved on its way, she'd told Mat. Finally, the pair flew over the rooftops of town, and Mat saw for the first time the antiquated but welcoming gas-lit lamps dotting town square and then his aunt's shop. As promised, there was a small window open in the attic.

CHAPTER 6

CATTITUDE ADJUSTMENT

For two days and nights, Shay prowled every inch of Havenwood Falls and the surrounding forests, searching for the fae who hid her prey. Her senses first took her to Coffee Haven, but neither the fae owner, one Willow Fairchild, nor her part-time barista, Paisley, held any trace of the man Shay sought. She discovered a few other children at the high school, including an elf as well as a distant relative to Willow according to Shay's magic, with no luck. It took her a while, but she eventually tracked down a tattoo artist who also possessed fae blood, but the girl was another dead end. How much Shay wished she could just make her dead, period. All fae, for that matter. The entire race had been her nemesis long before this mission ever began.

She consulted her locket regularly, thinking something must have changed, but its message never wavered. Until tonight.

Shay now sat on a bench in the middle of town square, her green gaze focused on the fountain at the center and the two tourists making wishes, but her senses were wide open to the surrounding area. She'd missed a faerie during her earlier investigations. This one had been gone for the last couple of days, and Shay hadn't been able to track her down. But as soon as she smelled the thing earlier in the evening, she recognized the scent from the coffee shop her first morning in town. The Broastful Brew, which she'd chosen at the time precisely because she didn't trust fae to serve her milk. If she'd only known the one keeping her from her heart's desire had been right under her nose that morning.

Not even the locket had known, though, which meant this . . . *creature* . . . had begun protecting the man some time that same day. The one whose shopfront read Madame Tahini's Potions, Lotions, Palm Readings, and Other Extra-Sensory Services. The faerie must have kept the man hidden under her disgusting fae magic. Even now, Shay couldn't go near the shop, which was protected by enchantments—not to mention the silver adorning every possible entrance. Not exactly Shay's favorite metal.

So here she sat, watching and waiting, listening and lingering, anticipating the arrival of the one who'd finally make her dreams come true.

She heard the flutter and whoosh of wings approaching and tilted her head back. A grin spread across her face as she saw them— a moth and an owl. Her heart exploded with emotion as she watched him soar overhead and into the shop's attic window.

The male half of the couple Shay had been watching witnessed the fly-by, as well.

"I guess Madame Tahini has bats in her belfry," the heavyset man commented to his wife, who was busily making wishes at the fountain.

Shay snorted as she stood up and sauntered away.

"I need a plan," she said aloud as she headed east toward her cabin. "It's been so long, and he probably remembers nothing. And I can't trust anyone else to do this if I want it done right. It'll have to be me."

She knew, however, that this man had an innocent soul, regardless of his true age and all he'd been through. His sweet trustful heart would get him into trouble one of these days. She needed to ensure she appealed to that wholesomeness if she wanted him to be hers. By the time she arrived at her cabin, she had a plan laid out, and she knew exactly where to start tomorrow.

CHAPTER 7

LAY OF THE LAND

*A*s usual, Teeny woke up shortly before sunrise and padded down to the kitchen-lab to brew a pot of tea. She poured a small cup and went to her salon. She saw a note had been slipped under the front door and was laying on the floor in the foyer.

She picked up the note and read the scrawled message:

Madame Tahini, my wife Gladys would like to have a reading before we leave Havenwood Falls, but you were not in today. Will come by tomorrow after lunch. Melvin & Gladys, Cleveland, TN

"Hmmm, guess I have to get back to work," she said aloud and frowned. She'd hoped to be able to show Mat the town, but he'd have to explore on his own.

Sipping her tea, she took a seat in the high-backed chair and gazed into the crystal globe. In the center floated miniature figures of a man and a woman sitting on lawn chairs beside a modest motorcoach plastered with numerous stickers from various states.

"Must be Melvin and Gladys," she mused aloud.

She waited as long as possible before going to Nina's at nearly ten a.m., knowing the seamstress was a night owl. As expected, Nina opened the back door with the slowness of a person who had just woken up.

"Ah, Teeny, good to see you." The Italian beauty welcomed her with a yawn. "Come in."

Teeny told Nina about her long lost nephew's arrival. Not everything, of course, with Nina being human and all. In fact, this version had Mat traveling through the Canadian Rockies and down to Colorado on foot.

"His clothes are now completely disheveled and ragged," she explained. "I need to have a couple of trousers and shirts made for him."

"Well, bring him in, and I will measure him up and dress the young man properly."

Now that can't happen. Teeny rubbed the back of her neck. "Well, he's had a really rough time with his traveling, and, you see, he's recuperating now. I don't think he can make it here just yet."

Nina eyed her for a long moment, and Teeny knew her friend probably saw right through her little white lie . . . well, for Teeny, any lie would be little and white. She giggled inappropriately at the thought, making Nina narrow her eyes with further suspicion. Teeny sobered up.

"Truth be told, his clothes literally fell off him in shreds, and, well, he's at my place butt-naked." She whispered these last words.

Nina's eyes widened.

"Oh, okay then," she finally said, seemingly satisfied. "See if you can describe him to me."

Teeny used herself in demonstration and comparison, and Nina took notes on a sketch pad.

"He must be quite large. Is he fat?"

Teeny laughed loudly. "No, he's just *big*! His mother's side of the family."

"Guess so. How tall is he?"

"Hmmm, a little less than a head taller than Barbie, I think."

Nina nodded then sketched out a model of a man in accordance with Teeny's description. Teeny agreed the proportions in Nina's drawing were correct.

Nina pulled out a bolt of lightweight denim and another of chambray. She had her own kind of magic—it occurred at the sewing machine. She came from a long line of tailors and seamstresses, all famed for their expert stitching and uncanny ability to create clothing in what seemed like only a matter of minutes.

In fact, it took Nina ninety minutes to measure, cut, and sew two trousers and two blue mottled shirts. Nothing fancy, but they would do the job of covering Mat for now. She told Teeny to bring Mat in when he was feeling better so she could measure him properly.

"I look forward to meeting him," Nina said with a smile as she placed the articles in a bag and handed it to Teeny.

Their eyes locked, and the smaller woman's finger tapped against her chin as a thought occurred to her. Yes, she most certainly needed to bring Mat in to meet Nina.

Mat was just waking up when Teeny walked in the door at nearly noon. She heard him stirring upstairs, so she hurried up with her packages. Teeny sat in her fortune teller's salon when he finally came down, dressed in a set of his new clothes. Not a bad fit, Teeny noticed with glee, considering Nina had never laid eyes on this customer. A little short in the length of the pants, but only by a hair. The pullover chambray shirt was near perfect.

She beckoned him to join her in a cup of tea.

"I could really use a cup of coffee. Do you have any, please?" Mathew asked.

"Not here, but I'll take you to Broastful Brew. There's also Coffee Haven, but I need to see the mayor, and I know I will find her at the Brew."

A few minutes later, the pair exited through the front door of Madame Tahini's shop. As they crossed the street and strolled through Town Square Park, Teeny pointed out the landmarks: City Hall directly across the square, flanked by the police station to the right and the Chamber of Commerce building to the left. Broastful Brew sat kitty-corner to the Chamber.

"The streets running from west to east are each named after an Old Family that founded Havenwood Falls," Teeny explained as they turned toward Broastful Brew. "This one in front of City Hall is named for the Stuarts, ancestors to the mayor."

Tahini introduced her nephew to Mabel, who immediately began to dote on him, fixing him her extra special macchiato and babbling on about how she couldn't wait for Macy, her part-time employee, to meet him. As expected, Teeny found the mayor sitting at their familiar table and led Mat over to her.

"Barbie, this is my nephew Mathew from Canada. He will be staying with me for a while."

Barbie eyed the young man, stood up, shook his hand, and said, "Pleasure to meet you." For the mayor, it was a pleasure to be able to look another in the eye without bowing her head. She then turned to Tahini with a raised eyebrow and said, "Don't recall a Mathew in the registry."

Tahini cleared her throat and whispered, "He's from the other side of the family, but I'll take care of it."

After Mathew had finished his caffeinated fix, Tahini suggested he explore the town on his own, since she had to prepare for her customers that were due at the salon.

"At the end of Memory Lane, the road behind my shop—"

"She means Beaumont Crossing Road," Mayor Barbie interrupted. Tahini shot her friend a glare. Barbie shrugged. "What? That's what the street sign says. You'll get him lost using names that no one's heard for over a century."

Teeny pursed her lips together in annoyance—more at the fact that the city council of ages ago had changed the street name than at her friend—before turning back to her nephew. "Anywho, at the end of the road there is Danzan Park. There's jogging paths, hiking trails, basketball courts, and much else to do. You might like it. Check it out."

Mat stood up from the table and shook the mayor's hand while

Teeny fumbled in one of her ubiquitous pockets and pulled out a few bills.

"In case you need it," she said as she handed him the fistful of money.

Before he started to depart the restaurant, Mat thanked Mabel for the sweet macchiato, and she practically swooned as he planted a gentle kiss on her hand. Teeny's brow dropped low over her eyes as she watched her nephew set out to survey the lay of the land, wishing she could accompany him.

After the familiar shopkeeper's bell noted Mat's exit, Mayor Barbie leaned over to Tahini, patted her hand, and spoke softly. "He's a big boy, Siobhan. Literally. In fact, not a boy at all. I'm sure he can handle our charming little town just fine."

Tahini looked at her with a raised brow. Barbie knew better than most how un-charming their little town could be. The mayor stared back at her friend and tilted her head.

"I think you aren't being completely forthright with me about your nephew, are you?"

"Are those troubling *visitors* still around?" was all Teeny replied. She wrinkled her nose at the faint trace of odor lingering on the air. "I can still smell them here."

"You mean those boisterous boy-men we saw here the other day?"

"Less boys or men, I think."

"Are you sure of this?"

"Are they still around?" Tahini repeated, and then a sudden thought hit her. "Oh my gods! I forgot to call Sheriff Kasun. There's a bloodless body in Gruff's grotto, and he's not very happy about it. He's been at my cabin for days now."

"There's been a body at your cabin for days now?" Barbie gasped.

"No! There's been a *troll* at my cabin for days now. The corpse is in the cave!"

"Oh, dear. Well, I'll let the sheriff know to check it out and to clean up for Gruff."

"Intuition tells me those boys have something to do with it, Barbie. Have they registered?"

The mayor's brows pinched together. "That's a good question. I'd have to check with Adelaide."

"Well, I'm pretty sure they need to," Teeny said pointedly. "The Court needs to be on top of that, because they may be dangerous."

Mat explored the town square, and by two p.m., he headed toward the park at the end of Memory Lane, aka Beaumont's Crossing Road. An ice cream gazebo sat at the entrance of the park, and several patrons stood around the tables shaded with colorful umbrellas while savoring their overstuffed cones. Mat licked his lips and decided he'd have ice cream as a late lunch.

As he made his way toward the order window, he couldn't help but notice the young woman standing by the bike rack. Her skin was white as snow, her cupid's bow lips a soft red, and her hair a shiny ebony, creating a contrast that he found stunning. She wore a pink top and leggings with an apple motif. She also wore a bright, shiny apple pendant at the base of her neck. She saw Mat looking at her, and her lips curled slightly in a demure smile as she dropped her gaze.

He walked up to the window to make his selection and put in his order.

"I recommend the apple cinnamon," a sweet voice said from behind him.

Mat turned to find the girl looking up at him through her long, dark lashes. Her fingers were wrapped around a waffle cone, black lacquered nails spotted with pink polka dots. Ice cream dripped over the cone's edge, and she licked her fingers with a soft pink tongue.

"I'm not surprised," Mat replied with an encouraging grin. "You seem to like apples."

She lifted her face and returned his smile. He was stunned by the lime green eyes that flashed at him.

"Are those contact lenses you're wearing?" he blurted.

The young woman looked into Mat's golden eyes and answered, "I might ask the same of you."

They exchanged smiles.

Mat held out his hand. "Hi, my name is Mat. Mat White."

Although not really his full name—his surname *meant* white warrior, but wasn't actually White—it had been what his father always gave during their travels. He'd said it was safer and also easier for people to say and spell than McFeeny. He didn't think this cute young woman could be dangerous, but using the pseudonym had become habit.

"I'm Shayin, but you can call me Shay," she said sweetly.

"Do you live here?" Mat couldn't take his eyes off the girl.

"No, here on vacation, staying in one of the cabin rentals in the mountains. The rates are very reasonable this time of year. How about you?"

"I'm new in town, and just starting to explore the area. I thought I'd walk through the park and check it out. Would you like to join me?"

Shay smiled a sweet, alluring smile and nodded. Mat ordered a double scoop of sassafras ice cream in a cake cone. It was much more to his liking than apple cinnamon, even though Shay had made it sound inviting.

The honey color already began to return to Mat's skin as he and Shay sauntered through the pathways of the town park, admiring the changing colors of the trees while continuing their getting-to-know-you banter along the way.

"Oh look!" Shay pointed with her left index finger. "I didn't know lunar moths were in this part of the country."

The pointed finger, unlike the other nine garnished with black and pink nail polish, sported a bandage at its tip.

"What happened to your finger?" Mat queried compassionately, distracting Shay from Cyllene's presence. He'd be embarrassed if she knew his aunt's sidekick was apparently checking up on him. After all, he wasn't a child.

Shayin quickly pulled her hand down and placed it behind her back.

"Oh that. Just a bicycle incident. I broke my nail when trying to change a tire."

∾

Buzzing madly once again, Cyllene was loud enough for Teeny to hear her from the salon. The Tennessee trippers had left after receiving the most informative reading of Gladys' spiritual ventures and paying Teeny handsomely for it.

Teeny went out into the garden, where she found Cyllene sulking on the water pump.

"So, what's the buzz, Silly Annie? Come on in, and I will set you up with a speaker."

Cyllene flew in through the open kitchen door and rested on the cupboard, while Teeny went to prep the table. She realized her only funnel was back at the cabin, so she pulled a roll of aluminum foil from a kitchen drawer and drew a large piece from it. She curled the foil into the shape of a cone and placed it atop a large coffee cup that sat on the table.

"Okay, now fill me in," she commanded.

The nymph settled behind the foil cone and began telling Tahini about Mat and the woman.

Like a song, Cyllene described them in poetic detail, Euterpe's spirit overflowing.

> La Femme Shayin, she's pale and thin.
> Her nails so long, but something's wrong.
> Black like claws, but do take pause.
> A bandage lingers on her left finger.
> L'Homme Mathew, has not a clue.
> Undoubtedly smitten with a raven-ish kitten.

"He met a girl already?" Teeny asked, though not surprised. Her nephew was handsome and sweet.

"Less a girl or woman," Cyllene said, and Teeny's brow shot high. She'd used a nearly identical phrase earlier with the mayor. Did Cyllene mean the same thing? "You said kitten . . ."

Cyllene nodded. "I believe so."

"Oh dear," Tahini said sullenly. A feline and a fowl were not exactly a perfect match. "Mat's heart may be in trouble."

"Maybe more than his heart," Cyllene added, a hint of fear in her tone.

CHAPTER 8

TIT FOR TAT, TAT FOR MAT

"*W*hy don't we go up to my place and get a refreshment?" Shayin purred as they finished the long hiking trail around Danzan Park and came to the bike rack by the ice cream hut.

"Sure, sounds great!" Mathew replied.

"Do you want to rent a bike, and we can pedal up to the cabin?" Shay suggested.

Mat loved that this beautiful girl was also athletic. Just the kind of woman he would want. He checked to see how much cash he had left, and there seemed to be an adequate amount for a bike rental.

Along with a receipt, the clerk gave Mat a brochure depicting the places in Havenwood Falls where he could drop off his rental. He met Shay back at the bicycle rack, and the two headed toward the mountain cabins. Mat was a little wobbly at first, but it seemed to be true that one never forgets how to ride a bike. They pedaled along the edge of town, enjoying the leaves of the aspens that lined the streets in their golden glory. A slight crisp autumn chill filled the air, keeping them cool even as their ride became more challenging once they were off-road, riding a trail up the mountain.

Once they arrived, Shay opened the door to the rental, revealing stylish Asian-contemporary furnishings, which were unexpected in a mountain cabin. Mat thought it comfortable enough for an extended vacation, but too sparse to encourage a longer engagement.

Mat took a seat on the futon sofa, while Shay went to the open kitchen to retrieve their refreshments.

"Would you like a glass of milk, Mat?" she offered.

Mat grimaced but politely responded, "No, thank you. Just water for me."

The sleek figure filled a glass with water, and then she retrieved a large mug that could be easily used as a bowl and filled that with milk. She brought the drinks over to the futon, handing Mat the glass and setting the cup on the coffee table. Shay slinked over to a sideboard and placed her phone on a docking station, sliding the icons over to her tunes and selecting a song. The room filled with music and the grandeur of Barbra Streisand's voice.

Shay took a seat on a pillow on the floor beside the coffee table and leisurely lapped the creamy liquid in her cup, making a low, soft vibrating sound as she swayed to the rhythm.

Mathew did not recognize the song, but said he liked the music.

"Ah, this is my favorite part."

And the voice from the small speakers boomed out about memories and moonlight and fatalistic warnings. Mat found it hauntingly beautiful.

The song ended and segued into a symphonic chorus, voices singing "up, up, up," and Shay patted the cushion next to her, inviting Mat to join her. He obediently took her cue and slid off the couch to her side. Shay stroked his beautiful mane, curling a strand of his brown-streaked, white-blond locks around a long, slender finger.

She whispered in his ear, almost purring. "I like you, Mat. Do you like me?"

"Mm-hmm," Mat responded.

The lanky legs of the woman curled around Mat's waist as her rough, warm tongue licked the nape of his neck. Her mouth made its way up his jaw and to his lips. She paused at the corner, her bright green eyes looking into his golden ones. She blinked slowly.

"Maybe we shouldn't," she whispered as she pulled slightly back.

Mat's hands lifted to her back and brought her closer. "It's up to you . . . but I want to."

She stared at him for a moment longer before she leaned in and brushed her lips against his. The kiss was soft and innocent at first, but quickly escalated as their mouths parted. Mat quickly realized she was much more experienced at this than he, her tongue stroking his teasingly, making his breathing grow heavy.

He began to remove his shirt, but before he knew it, Shay's fingernails ripped through the chambray, and the loose pullover fell from his back, revealing his smooth, caramel-colored skin with the dark scar across his shoulder blade. Shay traced the scar with her fingertip.

"Oooh, poor baby, did you have a bicycle accident too?" she cooed.

"No, I don't really know what happened. Something attacked me, but I didn't get to see what it was."

She smiled at him sweetly and pulled him closer to her to tenderly caress his scar.

Mat raised his hands to her small peaked breasts that filled his palms like a perfect fit. Shay gasped at the touch, but didn't pull back. In fact, she leaned into his hands, while she squirmed against his lap that was growing hard between them. He began to peck small kisses upon her throat and chest, and just as he was about to lift her top from her waistline, he noticed out the window that the sun had sunk much lower in the sky.

"Forgive me, Shay! I need to go." In one swift movement, he lifted her from his lap and set her down on the cushion before reaching for what remained of his shirt.

"*Go?* Are you kidding me? Go where?"

Mat floundered for a moment. "My aunt will be worried. I'm supposed to have dinner with her. Let's meet tomorrow, okay? Really, I'm very sorry. I like you a lot, I want you to know that."

"Sure, sure. I'll find you in town." She stood and wrapped her trim, lean arms around his neck, and the pair tasted their lingering passion on each other's lips.

"Tomorrow," she purred.

~

THE SUN CAST LONG, angled shadows as it set behind Mathew while he biked down the hill. At the bottom, he stopped long enough to check his brochure for a nearby drop-off. There appeared to be one on Beaumont's Crossing, and Mat remembered that was what his aunt called Memory Lane. He deposited his bicycle and ran down the lane to the back of Tahini's shop, swinging open the wooden gate and bounding through her overgrown garden. The back door was locked, and he banged on it fiercely.

Teeny swung the rear door open to find Mat sweaty and disheveled. He stepped through the threshold and quickly closed the door, locking it behind him and tossing his shirt on a chair at the table.

"Oh my gods, Mat, what happened?" She examined the tattered cloth that had been the kind craftsmanship of Nina.

Unable to answer, Mat stretched his arms out, and his transformation began. His skin turned to down, his legs shortened, and his jeans fell to his talons. His hoots, clicks, and trills began to tell Teeny about his day in the language of owls.

"Oh, my dear nephew, so you have a new friend. Her name is Shayin? Cyllene didn't seem impressed."

"What does a butterfly know about what a man needs?"

Teeny frowned. "Cyllene is not a butterfly. She is a nymph, and far older and wiser than you, young man, or should I say young owlet?"

Mat turned his owl head nearly full circle and back, hooting that there was no way that Shay was not a good woman.

"Just because she's beautiful doesn't mean she's bad. Cyllene is probably jealous," he retorted, remembering the beauty with whom he had just nearly shared his human flesh.

"She definitely has your body in mind, I'm sure. You are very handsome, and you don't even know it. You're definitely not practiced in the ways of these modern women. Just be careful!" Tahini continued to admonish.

"If she meant me any ill will, she certainly had the opportunity today. We have pheromones. Maybe there's even some owl in her," Mat mused.

His aunt frowned at him, but must have realized he would not be dissuaded from enjoying the company of his new friend.

"We will talk about this another time," Siobhan said. "Come on up to the attic. Just remember that your parents sent you here so I could keep you safe. That might mean from every vixen who sets her sights on you."

If Mat had been in his human form, he would've rolled his eyes, but in his owl form, he could only blink with his nictitating membrane. He perched himself on the shoulder of his tiny aunt as she went up the stairs and pulled down the attic access door for Mat to enter.

"We will go see Nina tomorrow, so that she can mend your shirt and do a proper fitting for you. Get some sleep. Please do not go out tonight." And with that, Mat flew into the attic, and Tahini pulled the rope to release the spring hitch that held the door in place. The access door lurched upward and shut with a loud thump.

MAT PADDED down from the attic around noon again the next day and found his teeny aunt in the laboratory-styled kitchen, cutting up herbs and placing them in the dehydrator. It appeared she had already completed a few bunches, as there was a pyramid of ground green powder next to her mortar and pestle.

"Good morning, Aunt Siobhan," he said as he planted a kiss on top of Tahini's head, bending nearly halfway over to do so.

"Morning? Try afternoon. We have a lot to do, so grab a cup of tea. There's plenty in the pot."

Mat obediently took a cup from the cupboard. His fingers too large to fit through the small handle, he held the cup in his palm as he poured the warm brew from the pot. He sat down to drink it as he watched his aunt busily preparing her powdered concoctions.

"As soon as I'm done with this catnip, we need to go over to Nina's and get that shirt repaired, as well as have her fit you for more appropriate wear, especially since the weather is changing. Then we have to go the Court of the Sun and the Moon and register you ASAP."

She ground more dried catnip in her mortar while Mat finished his tea, then the man-owl stood up and took his tattered shirt from the chair he had thrown it on last night. He eyed it with regret.

"I'm sorry about the shirt, Aunt Siobhan."

"No worries, honey. Nina is a whiz. She'll fix it. Are you ready?"

Mat bobbed his head in an owl-like nod, and the two exited the rear of Teeny Weeny's townhome.

They arrived at Nina's Dress Perfect Havenwood Falls shop at about one o'clock in the afternoon, just as Nina was opening up. Nina's eyes widened as her gaze traveled down the man before her and slowly back up, causing Mat to blush. He couldn't help but give her the same once-over, making him wonder how so many beautiful women could exist in one little town. When his appreciative stare came to her face, their eyes locked—his golden ones ensnared by her dark brown orbs. Something passed between them that he could not identify, but sent a jolt through his body. His Aunt Siobhan cleared her throat, as though reminding them they were not alone, breaking the connection.

"Oh, please, do come in," Nina hurriedly said as her blush deepened.

The trio entered the shop, and Nina instructed Mat to stand by the mirror, as she retrieved her tape measure and placed her wristband pin cushion on her arm. She first measured his height at 6'5" and then his inseam at 34.5", and each time she touched him, Mat's heart skipped a beat.

"Now for your wingspan," Nina said, not realizing the truth of her comment. Teeny and Mat just smiled at each other.

After taking Mat's full measure, the olive-skinned seamstress went over to the bolts of fabric in a myriad of colors.

"I'd like a black shirt, maybe," Mat volunteered when he noticed her gaze sweeping over all the choices. He didn't particularly care, but black seemed an easy choice, the first color to pop in his mind as he recalled the softness of Shay's hair. He hoped he'd see her again today.

"Black? What are you, Mafioso? Cosa Nostra?" Nina responded in her lyrical Italian accent.

"Give him something a bit more colorful, Nina," his aunt said. "There's enough blackness in this life as it is."

Nina picked out several bolts of cloth, one that was a mosaic of colors fixed in odd geometrical shapes like a stained-glass window, another a sateen brownish gold that would highlight the streaks in his hair. She also picked out a more sedate pinstriped cotton material, for dressier occasions.

"Bene! Let me fix that tattered top now," Nina said as she took the damaged garment from Teeny, who had been holding it all this time.

Nina examined the tears in the shirt. "Hmm, this looks awfully vicious. Like un gatto."

"It was all just playing around with a friend I met. Nothing serious," Mat replied defensively.

Nina found a few swatches of the light denim she had used to create Mat's trousers and cut them to form patches. She craftily applied the patches to the ripped cloth with beautiful tiny stitches, leaving the shredded edges of the shirt as a stylistic touch. The pullover now appeared as though it'd been originally designed to have a worn look.

"Nina, you are a magician!" Mat vigorously complimented the slender beauty. "Thank you!"

"Nessuna magia, solo abilità," Nina replied proudly, tossing her brunette braid to the side with a smile. She translated, "No magic, just skill. I will have some proper shirts and slacks for you in a few days. I will let Teeny know when they are ready."

Tahini hugged her talented friend and led Mat out of Nina's shop with his newly repaired shirt.

"Nina is so talented," Tahini said as they walked down the street. "And beautiful, too."

"Yes, she is both," Mat agreed.

"I saw the way she looked at you," Teeny hinted.

Mat blushed. "Aunt Siobhan, are you already trying to set me up?"

"Isn't that part of my job?" she said, and Mat couldn't tell if she teased or truly believed that. "Nina's a nice girl."

"I met a nice girl yesterday. I hope to see her again."

They paused at the street corner before crossing. "Well, one can't have too many friends, now can they?"

Then she let the subject drop.

⁓

TAHINI LED Mat across the street and around to the back of City Hall, down a short flight of steps to a door that appeared to be a service entrance to the building. A metal door welcomed them, emblazoned with an emblem of a sun and a moon.

Tahini rapped on the service entrance door. Tap, tap, tap, pause, tap, tap, pause, tap, tap, tap, tap.

The door swung open, and a woman wearing a black hooded sweatshirt and ripped-up jeans, holding something that looked like an airbrush but with a seriously sharp needle, welcomed them in. The young woman peered through her black-framed glasses as she gave Mathew a once-over.

"This is my nephew who has come to stay with me, and I need to register him. So please prepare a tattoo for Mathieu," Tahini explained, pronouncing Mathieu like Mat-too for the rhyme she so much loved to create.

Adelaide Beaumont, or Addie, as the younger set called her,

served as the registrar for the Court of the Sun and the Moon. She led the two toward a desk in the back of a large room that resembled a courtroom, with a raised dais in the front facing the gallery. She withdrew a form from the middle drawer of the desk and handed it to Mat, along with a pen.

From the side drawer, Addie took out a push pin that was hermetically sealed and a small petri dish and placed them on the top of the desk. After Mat finished filling out his form and handing it back to the registrar, the woman removed the push pin from its safety wrapper and requested Mat hold out his right hand. She pricked his finger and squeezed a few drops of Mat's blood onto the petri dish.

Addie covered the dish and left the room.

"What was that for?" Mat inquired.

"It's part of the registration process," Tahini explained. "The Court maintains strict protective measures for the town's residents. They want to know about you and what kind of supernatural blood you have. In turn, Addie will infuse the tattoo she'll give you with magic specially created so you can exist safely in Havenwood Falls."

Addie returned with a tray of colorful inks and reported that Mat was part spring faerie and part owl-shifter, the owl-shifter being quite rare in Havenwood Falls. She really didn't know much about them. Mat explained that his mother's was the owl-shifter side of the family, and they were the guardians of the woods to protect the faerie families.

"Tell me more," Addie said as she took out her sketch pad and began drawing.

Mat told her how his father Seamus, Siobhan's uncle, met his mother Abigail in Wales some six centuries or so ago. They were forced to evacuate as the bubonic plague ravished the country and both the faeries and the owl-shifters were accused of causing the Black Death.

Addie looked up at him, pausing in her sketch. "I didn't know that."

"Well, the plague was actually caused by fleas," Tahini

interjected. "But there was much misunderstanding at the time. Many foolish folk interpreted fleas as anything small and flying, include faeries. Others misinterpreted the bubonic by thinking *bubo* was for the owls."

Addie nodded before adding a few final strokes to her creation, then she lifted the pad and turned it for Mat and Teeny to see. She'd drawn an intricate design with the shape of an owl as its center theme, and it looked remarkably like the crest on the family album Tahini and Mat had pored over just a few days before. Tahini had told her nephew on the way over that Addie was an "artiste extraordinaire," and Addie's illustration proved her point.

Mat beamed with approval, and Addie set forth with the task of applying a tattoo to his forearm while asking more questions about Mat's background.

"My mum and dad's families both evacuated to the small island of Gwynf'l. It's off the shores of England, Wales, and Ireland," Mat said as she pressed the needle into his skin. He shared the same story his parents had told him, about how they lived peacefully for hundreds of years alongside a few fishermen and their families in the tiny village at the base of the mountains. He was the youngest of his siblings, born only 70 years ago. His brother and sister took after the fae side of the family, and he was the only owl-shifter other than his mother, Abby. Fortunately, on the isle of Gwynf'l, the serenity of the place made it easy for his mother to be the sole guardian of the faeries.

"Until, of course, I was born," Mat said. "But even then, I didn't come of age until I was fifty, and I'm still not fully mature, since I can't yet shift at will."

Addie seemed to enjoy the story, and by the time Mat finished, so had she. Teeny and Mat left the Court, Mat admiring the workmanship that now adorned his arm.

"Would you like to set me up with Addie, too, Aunt Siobhan?" Mat teased after they left.

Teeny laughed. "She's a pretty girl, too, but definitely not your type. She has a bad boy complex."

They rounded the corner of City Hall and faced town square.

"It's getting pretty late, and soon you'll be shifting. Why don't we go to The Haven Saloon for happy hour, then we can make sure you're set up for the night," Teeny suggested as she glanced up at the sky. While the sun began its descent over Miles Mountain to the west, foreboding clouds rolled over Mt. Mae's peaks to the south.

Mat nodded in agreement, and they both crossed the town square and walked in through the batwing doors of the saloon. They blinked as their eyes adjusted to the darker atmosphere. Two large picture windows flanked the doors, allowing a bit of the late afternoon sun to slant inside, but the natural light only reached so far, giving way to dimly lit pendulum lamps and wall sconces. The long, gleaming wooden bar stretched down one side of the room, with tables and booths dotting the rest of the space. The décor was a bit rustic, showing its old-time roots, mixed with touches of industrial chic that gave it a modern flair. With smoke swirling around him, Bent Brent stood behind the bar this afternoon, as per usual, and greeted the pair.

"Madame Tahini," Brent said in his laid-back voice. "What a pleasure to see you. And who is this handsome specimen you have with you?"

Tahini introduced Mathew as they selected a couple barstools near the center of the bar. Brent handed Tahini a fat cushion from under the bar, and Teeny placed it on the seat before climbing onto the stool. Brent always kept the booster handy for her, even though her appearances at the tavern were infrequent.

The saloon was bustling this afternoon. Teeny spotted three of the pixie sisters sitting at a high-top table near the back of the bar, all of them with hurricane glasses nearly as big as their heads, filled with colorful liquids and sporting tiny paper umbrellas. Aeiri was at the bar, flirting with Brent. Their own marks required by the Court glamoured them into appearing human while out and about in town, but their smaller-than-average frames and their colorful clothes and ribbons made them look like they belonged on the playground rather than in a bar.

She recognized the boisterous boys from the Brew at a table in the far corner of the room. If she hadn't seen them, she couldn't miss their stink, even over that of spilled beer and Bent Brent's smoke. They were still as loud and obnoxious as before, making crude jokes to anyone who would listen.

The Haven Saloon catered to both the human and supernatural varieties of the town. It specialized in martinis mainly for the human beings, and the entire bottom row of bottles behind the bar were varying flavors of vodka, from Apple to Zucchini—yes, even zucchini for the veggie fanatics that ventured to imbibe.

The top shelf held an interesting array of wine bottles, all labeled with Stone Falls Winery, the local vineyards, but each with a different name and flavor. Not all meant for humans.

"I'll have one of your wonderful virgin mojitos, Brent." Tahini ordered her favorite. Mat was still perusing all the interesting labels while the bartender began to mix his special virgin cocktail for Tahini, which he knew she liked with ginger ale. Tahini, due to her own stature, did not partake in alcoholic libations, as even an ounce of the fermented variety would throw her for a loop.

Brent placed the refreshing mint-infused drink in front of Teeny. Mat opened his mouth to order when he glanced down the bar and stopped abruptly. Teeny looked up from the swirling drink she had been sipping on and followed his bright gaze to the young woman with black hair and pale white skin, wearing a pink sweater, white pants, and a shiny red apple pendant on her chest. She recognized the woman as one of Mabel's favorite new regulars at Broastful Brew.

The girl batted her eyelashes and waved her fingers in a flirtatious way at Mat. Teeny noticed her nails—all but one, anyway —were quite long and sharp, a contrast to the rest of her sweet and innocent appearance. She suddenly understood what had happened to Mat's shirt yesterday. *Sweet and innocent, my ass,* Teeny thought, and she tried not to imagine what kinds of ways the beauty had tried to corrupt her Mathew, whom she wanted to believe was as pure as snow was white.

"I'll have what that beautiful woman at the end of the bar is having," Mat said to Brent, though he didn't remove his gaze from the girl.

"I don't think so, young man, judging by your tattoo. She's drinking Owl's Overture," Brent informed him. "How about Rabbit's Run? I think you will find that much more to your liking."

Bent Brent poured Mat a goblet of Rabbit's Run Zinfandel blend from Stone Falls Winery, placed it before the young man, and took a hit from the joint he had stoking by the register. Brent didn't mind serving all of the unusual characters that came to the saloon, as long as they didn't mind his own version of relaxation. He returned his attention to the fiery pixie at the bar, who was now sitting next to Tahini.

"I'm going to join Shay for a moment," Mat informed his aunt as he picked up his glass of wine.

Tahini looked at the pendulum clock that hung at the back of the bar under the loft. "Not too long. Look at the time. We will have to dash in a bit."

Mat nodded at his aunt and tipped his glass toward Shay. He smiled his alarmingly beautiful smile, and Shay grinned back. She did not move from her chair, but patted the stool next to her. Invitation accepted, Mat took a seat next to the charming woman.

"Bartender, could you bring us a couple of shots of Luscious Red Apple Schnapps?" asked the woman Mat had called Shay.

Brent obliged the pretty lady, then he and Teeny engaged in their typical catching up with recent and past history of Havenwood Falls. Each with their own unique take on the past, they laughed as she sipped and he smoked.

Tahini picked up on the sudden movement to her right, just a second before the sound of broken glass filled the saloon. She felt little pin-pricks in her skin as the glass shards scattered across the bar and floor. She looked over to ensure Mat was okay. Somehow, Enya was already over there, standing on the bar over Mat and Shay. Mat's mouth hung agape as he stared at the woman's breasts while the liquid dripped down her pale skin and stained her pink sweater a deeper shade of red.

Brent, the good barkeep he was, moved quickly with his towel to assist the lovely maiden, now in distress, and began to pat the liquid off her breast.

Chairs were heard hitting the floor as the boy twins jumped out of their seats to join the commotion. Shay shot the twins an evil eye, even as they seemed to be coming to her rescue.

One of the boys grabbed Brent by the neck collar, while the other one grabbed Mat's arm and whirled him around on the swivel stool, lifting his fist in the air threateningly.

The batwing doors of the saloon flew open, and the large muscular frame of Sheriff Kasun filled the entryway.

"What's all this ruckus?" the sheriff bellowed as he took in the sight of what looked to be the start of a bar brawl.

Aeiri and Ushka were apologizing to anyone who would listen, while pretending to clean up the shards from their sister's clumsiness.

Meanwhile, Enya returned to Teeny's side and whispered in her ear, "I saw her put something in Mat's apple shot. I kicked it out of his hand."

Teeny nearly fell off her stool with surprise. She didn't know what was going on, but she needed to get Mat out of there.

The sheriff strode down to the four men at the end of the bar, ready to kick ass now and take names later.

"You gentlemen want to settle down?" he asked, in a tone that was more demanding then polite.

The one clenching Brent's collar let loose of his hold, and the other dropped his hand from Mat's freshly tatted arm. The wolf smell emitting from the ferocious-looking sheriff might have caused the two to backpedal.

Teeny saw her opportunity and jumped up. "Mat, we should go! You don't need trouble with the sheriff."

She bustled to the end of the bar and folded her hand over Mat's, tugging him toward the exit. Mat glanced at the soaking Shay forlornly and shrugged his large shoulders as they left.

Tierri and Enya walked them out, and Teeny heard Tierri say, "Well, wasn't that fun!"

Tahini knew all of the sisters would be reenacting that scene for some time to come.

As soon as they returned to Tahini's shop, Mat went upstairs to sulk, and a knock on the door brought Teeny back to it. Sheriff Kasun's large body filled the entry, the sky behind him already darkening with ominous clouds.

"I promise you Mat had nothing to do with it," she said.

"I know. I came to tell you about the body you reported in the cave. We didn't find anything, but I recognized a scent in the cave as the same on those boys."

"I knew they were bad news!" Teeny said.

"We have nothing solid to go on now, but we'll be keeping our eyes open and our noses to the ground."

CHAPTER 9

THE BALL TELLS ALL

*L*ightning flashed and thunder boomed overhead as Teeny took her favored seat at the round table of her salon. Mat still hadn't come out of the attic, so she'd gone up to check on him. He'd been perched on an old dresser, watching the storm out the window, his owl eyes looking as forlorn about the weather as his human ones had when they'd left the bar. He had it bad for that woman, but Teeny questioned her motives. She trusted Enya, who had no reason to lie about the poison, but why in the fae would anyone want to poison sweet Mathew?

She bent over the colorful globe with its galactically swirling lights. She'd tried to reach her uncle the day before, after her clients had left, but with no luck. Now, with the terrible thought that someone might have tried poisoning her nephew, she had to speak with him. Using the ball to connect with his matching one was the only way to reach him, the link between the spheres serving as a private family network that didn't rely on cell signals and phone numbers, or anything else of the human world.

The faerie waved her hands over the globe as it took on hues of green and she uttered, "Tahini McFeeny, Famous Seamus," repeating the phrase several times as the green hues grew more vibrant and a face began to appear in the glass.

A rich baritone voice came from the ball. "Siobhan! If you have summoned me, it means that Mathew found you. Bless the fae!"

The kind face of her uncle looked up at her through the portal glass, so much like her own loving father's face, it made her cringe with remembrance.

"Seamus, he has! He made it, but a little worse for the wear when he first arrived." She saw her uncle frown and hurried to add, "He is fine now. Why didn't you tell me he was coming?"

"Mat's in danger. We felt he would be safer with you in . . . that town . . . I don't remember its name. We told him to fly to Colorado, but we couldn't remember exactly where, so we said to search for waterfalls, and when he felt the pull in his owl's soul, he would know he was near."

"That was so risky. Thank goddess we even found each other!"

"Yes, bless the fae. Again! We've been running nigh these past two decades from the Pisiks. Mother and I were worried if we forewarned you, the wrong folk may get wind of it."

"Well, I think your *someones* did get wind of it, and I think they are here in Havenwood Falls. Why?"

Seamus McFeeny began to tell Teeny the story. "It started some twenty years ago on our island of Gwynf'l. You do remember the homeland?"

Teeny nodded emphatically, recalling her ancestral lands.

"So two decades ago, the Pisik Coven had come upon the island disguised as a band of nomadic gypsies," Seamus continued in his formal yet rambling way of speaking. "They added a little spice to the lonely fishermen's wives and children. The townspeople were completely naïve to the clan's cat-shifting ways and their black magic."

"Black magic?" Teeny repeated with a gasp. She shook her head. "But what does this have to do with Mat?"

Seamus frowned again, and Teeny could see the deep lines etched in his forehead through the mystical globe.

"Mat witnessed one of their rituals," he finally said in a whisper, as though afraid the wrong ears would hear him. "When he came back to the aerie and told us of the events he had seen, we knew we had to leave our lovely island. The Pisiks, especially Shayin—she's the daughter of the high priestess and a Greater Pisik—are relentless, and Mathew wasn't going to be safe here, or maybe anywhere for that matter."

"Well, what did he see?" Teeny demanded.

Seamus's face wavered in and out of view. "It is too terrible to say. We wiped the event from Mat's memory, because nobody should remember the horrors he told us. Has something happened there?"

Teeny could hear the fear in her uncle's voice. She tried to curl her lips up in a reassuring smile. "Nothing for you to worry about, dear uncle. I'll take care of it."

Needing answers, Tahini resolved to do some research on these Pisiks, and the gruesome rituals they performed, so she returned to her salon library. It had been a long day, and Teeny was weary, and grateful the book she was seeking was on the lowest shelf, appropriately.

"Closer to hell, where you belong," she muttered to herself.

The book was completely black with only the letters ABC on the spine. She dreaded to even touch it, but knew it would give her the answers she required.

She settled into her high-back chair and opened the book to the title page: "Art of the Black Covens."

Scanning through the table of contents, she found "Pisik Coven" at Chapter 13. Tahini flipped to the appropriate page, and her belly fluttered with nerves as she saw this chapter devoted specifically to the Pisik Coven, and their dreadful procedures:

AMONG THE MOST *sinister of all Black Covens is by far the Pisiks, black magic practitioners who have mastered the art of transmogrification. The Pisik mages tend to choose large cats as their familiars, shifting into those forms for both utility and pleasure. The Pisik clan originated in ancient Persia, but after crossing the Black Sea into Romania, they became more nomadic, with a mixture of cats beyond the leopard and lynx of their homeland.*

The Coven is led by a High Priestess and a High Priest. Under them are the Greater and Lesser Pisiks. Those with a pure bloodline through the High Priestess and High Priest's consummation are the Greater Pisiks. This bloodline enables the Pisik to shift shape into its totem cat at will, whenever and wherever. The Lesser Pisiks can only shift at night, and some only during the week of the full moons.

Nearly every ritual of the Pisiks, from the simplest spells to the quite complex, contain some form of blood sacrifice, whether it be human, animal, or even supernatural. Their uses of these rituals are oftentimes for mere play and are not truly for any useful purpose, much like a cat will play with a bird or a mouse until it has been completely mutilated, though the cat has no intention of eating the poor creature.

The goriest of their rituals is the Resurrection Blood Ritual, which can only be performed during the peak of the Blood Moon, and which requires the sacrifice of a human female virgin. If the virgin is of tender years, they only require the child's blood to transfer the life force. However, if more advanced, such as an adolescent or young adult virgin, an additional organ would be required, a liver or kidney. Their most extreme form of this ritual is when they have acquired a mature virgin, such as a nun. In this case, they would not only blood let, but they would rip the heart out of the sacrificial virgin, while it still quivered with minimal life, and eat from the meat of the organ.

TEENY'S NOSE wrinkled at the thought of eating a heart—or any other animal organ.

"What kind of evil does such a thing?" she wondered aloud before continuing with the passage.

IT WOULD SEEM to unknowing readers that at least this ritual had a purpose. However, the Pisik Coven might perform this ritual only so they could resurrect a prey they had previously enjoyed to repeat the kill.

Their blood rituals were first derived based on the full moons. In fact, while human children learned the names of the months, Pisik children learned the names of the moons: Wolf, Hunger, Crow, Fish, Milk, Rose, Thunder, Sturgeon, Harvest, Blood, Beaver, and Cold Moons.

As their blood thirst developed over the centuries, they began to create rituals for the new moons, then the half-moons. All, of course, entailing some sort of blood-letting.

The fact that the Pisiks will even sacrifice a supernatural is, perhaps, the reason they are deemed the most wicked coven. They perform this ritual annually on the last full moon of the year, the Cold Moon, attributing their longevity to this sacrifice. Once they've identified the chosen prey, they keenly observe it to determine its weaknesses, in order to overcome the creature for their ritual. Vampires are their favorite prey, most likely because of the enriched blood of the vamp, especially after it has just recently dined.

Identifying a Pisik member is not difficult. Because they are an ancient breed with a very tight-knit bloodline, they carry strong characteristics. The Pisiks have a very stealthy walk, with an appearance of stalking. Their footfalls are nearly soundless. All have raven-colored hair and pale skin. The Lesser Pisiks, typically leopard shifters, may have splotchy skin, depicting the remnants of their spots. The females have uncannily long black fingernails. In older times, this trait made it very easy to identify them, but with the fashion lacquers of modern days, it no longer acts as the tell-tale sign. In fact, a Pisik may actually paint their nails a different color simply to hide this unusual pigmentation. At least one of these black claws on the Greater Pisiks is made of iron.

TEENY GASPED AGAIN SO LOUDLY, it was almost a screech. The iron thorn in Mat's shoulder had not been a thorn after all! She was so distraught over what her poor nephew had been through, she almost missed a very important line:

. . .

THE BEST WAY TO subdue a Pisik is with catnip.

TAHINI CLOSED the book with a heavy sigh and an even heavier heart. How would she explain to her nephew that the reason his family had been running for so long the deceptively sweet, pretty young woman he'd taken such a liking to? Even more importantly, how was she going to protect him against such evil magic?

Good thing she'd already been grinding catnip and had a lot more in her healthy backyard garden!

She turned her chair 180 degrees to face the wall behind her. She pulled on the bottom corners of a small tapestry, and a drop-down door revealed a recess in which her computer was stored. Teeny tapped in her password on the keyboard. Once the machine came alive with her apps, she clicked on the folder called "Sky Charts." She opened the Moon file, and using her mouse cursor like a finger, she traced along the navigational lines.

"Oh my gods!" she shrieked when she saw that the Hunter's Moon, aka Blood Moon, was scheduled to peak tomorrow.

Whatever this Pisik woman had planned for Mat, Teeny knew mages well enough to conclude the time had come—she'd make her move under the Blood Moon.

CHAPTER 10

A PLAN FOR THE MAN

*S*hayin stalked across the porch of her log cabin, still fuming about the events in the bar earlier in the day. She'd been so close to finally obtaining what she'd been after for so long! But those bumbling idiot twins had nearly ruined everything. Well, first, there was the woman who'd jumped on the bar. Shay didn't know what she and her sisters—they had to be sisters judging by their likenesses—were even doing in the saloon. They looked like they belonged in school. Nonetheless, the one was apparently a jealous sort and had a thing for Mat, because she'd knocked the drink right out of Mat's hand and all over *her* chest.

"Stupid little girl!" Shay shouted out loud. "You have no idea what you're getting in the middle of."

And those dumb brothers. Shay slammed her fist on the porch railing. She didn't need protecting, especially from them, and she really didn't need the sheriff's attention, at all. Yet their testosterone-induced need for a bar brawl had definitely brought it. When the sheriff had mentioned to her a town registry for visitors, she'd promised she would take care of it first thing.

Of course, she couldn't care less about their stupid laws. If he only knew whom he was talking to! It didn't matter, though. She wouldn't be around much longer anyway.

The sun had been about to set, and a storm brewed over the mountain, sending everyone scurrying for shelter. Lightning now shot across the sky, and thunder cracked right after it. Rain poured down through the trees, heavy enough for some to reach the ground. Mat wouldn't be out in this weather tonight, and Shay was running out of time.

She performed the spell to consult the presence in her locket, chanting:

> Heart of Darkness on this chain,
> Holder of answers, do proclaim!
> Your eye is sagacious, sharp, and shrewd,
> Tell me what you know is true!

The red mist rose and the voice replied:

> Greater Pisik, Lady Shayin
> Master of darkness that flows within
> The Blood Moon comes on the morrow
> And by its light you may end your sorrow.
> But you must be cunning, stealthy, and wise
> To capture your prey before the moonrise.
> If in this task, you should fail
> Cursed you'll forever be to weep and wail

Shay snapped the locket closed. "Again with your stupid advice."

She stared at the charmed charm and its apple shape, and a new plan began to form.

CHAPTER 11

BLOOD MOON RISING

Tahini had gone to bed filled with dread, but as soon as she woke the next morning, she had a plan. While the high schoolers decorated the town square outside for their big game this weekend—if they won, they'd proceed to the playoffs—Teeny set forth to prep the cabin. The cabin was to be a fortress for her and Mat during the full moon, protecting them from any sick blood rituals any evil creatures might have in mind.

She filled an enormous carpetbag she had purchased at Callie's Consignments years ago with a few frocks, several scarves, a wool jacket knitted by Nina, and the garments Nina had completed for Mathew. Though she hardly ever traveled, she fell in love with the nineteenth-century luggage, which seemed to be a good match with the tapestries she fondly hung on her studio walls. It was much like the bag seen in Disney's "Mary Poppins," and since it was Tahini's, just as magical. Callie had told her that she was sure the travel bag's previous owner was none other than Phileas Fogg. Teeny giggled at the story, not revealing to Callie that Phileas Fogg was a fictional character, but what a great name.

Tahini collected several mason jars of the catnip powder she'd been grinding. She also plucked out of the earth a few extra catnip plants that she intended to transplant around the cabin for extra measure.

Teeny went to her computer and checked the Sky Chart one more time. Sunset was to occur at 6:48 p.m. Checking the digital clock in the bottom corner of her computer screen, it was now nearly 10 a.m. She had fewer than nine hours before the Blood Moon would rise in its full glory, and another twelve hours before the sun would rise again on game day. Mat woke up earlier than usual, since he hadn't been able to hunt the night before, and Teeny sent him out to help the kids with the decorations.

She solicited Cyllene's help, who was always eager to assist, and given Cyllene's limited abilities, her primary chore was to keep watch over Mat. She was to let Siobhan know if the woman at the bar came anywhere near him. Cyllene reported throughout the day that she had not seen the woman or the two boys anywhere in town, or the park or even the great falls. One would think this announcement would ease Teeny's mind, but instead, she became more worried. Since her reading of the Pisik rituals, she was concerned that the disappearance of the Pisik woman only meant the black mage was busying herself with her evil plans to sacrifice her dear nephew. There was not much time.

Teeny shimmered to the cabin and back to prepare it appropriately. She planted some of the catnip sprouts around the cabin and set the jars of brownish-green powder, one on the table, another in the loft on her steamer-style chest, and a third near the pot-bellied stove. She also kept one in her pocket at all times, just in case.

By two o'clock in the afternoon, the town square had been elegantly adorned with all manner of streamers, banners, and balloons strewn throughout, and Teeny's preparations had been completed.

"Meet us at the cabin, Silly Annie," she said when the nymph came in for her final report at the town home. Cyllene circled Tahini's head three times and flew off to the northwestern end of the canyon toward the cabin.

Teeny brought some herbs and lavender into the kitchen, wrapped them in a swatch of cheesecloth, and bent over to stuff them in her carpetbag sitting on the floor. When she straightened up, there was Mat, beaming at her.

"Hi, Aunt Siobhan. Decorating was fun, but we're done."

"Oh, good! Last night's storm reminded me that we need to go up to the cabin to prep it for the winter." It was a half-lie, because this is the time of year she began to shore up the cabin to prevent any damage from the heavy winter snowfalls that would be coming soon enough. She'd tried to warn Mat this morning about his new crush, but he refused to believe Shayin could possibly mean him any harm, so Siobhan stopped mentioning her.

"I can't fit in your cabin," he reminded her.

"You can help around the outside. There's much to do," she assured. "I'm going to shimmer us there so we have more time before sunset. Ready?" she asked.

With a drop of his shoulders, he nodded. Teeny instructed him to pick her up, while she held the carpetbag, and she would take it from there. He did as he was told, she wrapped her arms around his neck, and the two of them began to ripple into a translucent screen, and then disappeared from the kitchen of Number 19 Main Street.

The ripple effect re-appeared outside of Teeny's cabin.

"Oh crap!" Teeny screamed, as Cyllene buzzed nervously around her and Mathew's heads. "We hit a major stipple in the ripple."

The sun, which had been much higher in the sky, was already nearing its descent behind Miles Mountain to the west.

"This has to be at least a three-hour time lapse! It must be due to carrying all the extra luggage. Sorry, Mat, no offense. I was hoping we'd have a few hours of daylight to get things in order. Let me go up to the loft and open the windows so you can get in the cabin by twilight."

Teeny unlocked the cabin, and she and Cyllene entered the rustic abode. Cyllene immediately flew to the funnel and began crying out, "Oh my gods, Siobhan, I was so afraid for you and Mat! It took you so long, and the pixies, Gruff, and I were looking for you all over the mountain and falls. We thought maybe the panther got you or something."

"You've seen the panther?" Teeny asked. "Here in the woods?"

"Yes! Over by Gruff's cave!"

Teeny Weeny Tahini, despite her size, generally feared little, but now her heart began to pound. Her nephew could be in grave danger.

"I wasn't expecting to lose this much time! It's never been this large of a lapse, but then, I've never carried anything quite as large as Mat, either. In any case, let's get this place ready for the night. We have less than an hour before the Blood Moon begins to rise."

MAT STOOD OUTSIDE THE CABIN, watching the warm colors of orange and purple painting the sky both east and west with the brush of the setting sun. In the last remnants of the pale blue sky overhead, now beginning to darken around the edges, a few stars glimmered brightly. His owl nudged against his skin, ready to take control for the night.

Above him, Teeny opened the loft window and popped her head out. "As soon as you turn, fly into the cabin PDQ. The girls saw a panther nearby."

Not having a spectacular experience with wildcats in the past, Mat fully planned to obey his aunt, but just as he lifted his arms upward, feathers sprouting along his skin, something shiny and red on the ground caught his eye.

"Shay," he half-whispered, half-chirped as his amber gaze swept the area around him. Knowing how much she loved her apple pendant, considering how she wore it all the time, he forced himself toward it even as his body began the change. What was it doing on the ground in the woods? Was she okay? *The panther*, he thought with a panic, one of his last as a human. His next was, *Are those eyes in the trees?* He heard the spine-tingling growls at the same time his feathered fingertips grasped for the pendant.

As soon as he touched it, everything went black.

~

TEENY HURRIED outside and sprinkled the dried, ground catnip on the front porch and around the house, her nose wrinkling when she caught the foul odor on the air, the stench now familiar.

"Feral cat," she said aloud, finally pinpointing the musky smell she'd first caught in Broastful Brew and then in The Haven Saloon. A moment later, she caught the unmistakable scent of a large, female feline and gasped. "A black panther named Shay!"

She ran around the cabin as the bit of fear from earlier grew, causing her heart to pound wildly. Her wide eyes scanned the surrounding woods as she ran, but not seeing what she sought, she rushed back inside.

"Mathew," she called as she tilted her head back to try to see him up on the loft. Cyllene fluttered down, having finished lighting candles throughout the cabin.

"He hasn't come in yet," the nymph said once she alit at the funnel.

"He wasn't outside, either. But the panther has been!"

The pixies came running into the cabin, shouting, "The cat has Mat! The cat has Mat!"

"Where?" Teeny demanded.

"That way!" All four pixie sisters pointed in a different direction.

Teeny pressed her lips together. "We will have to take to the sky and search them out, Cyllene."

"We will take to the ground," Tierri said.

"No. You stay here. It's too dangerous," Teeny said.

"You cannot go alone! Safety in numbers, remember?" Ushka crossed her arms over her chest.

"Use your faerie dust," Cyllene said.

Tahini frowned. She didn't like the idea of all of her friends risking their lives, but she didn't have time to argue, either, especially with four pixies and a nymph. With a sigh, she retrieved a silk pouch from her pocket and poured out a small pile of sparkling pink dust into her palm. She faced the pixies and blew. As soon as the sisters began to lift from the ground, all color drained from Teeny's hair and skin, tiny bubbles fizzed and popped, and in a moment, she was like a white bullet, ready to shoot through the air and find her nephew Mathew.

MAT CAME to in his Bubo scandiacus form, his wings stretched out with painful stabs shooting through them. He turned his head to inspect his appendages, but saw nothing wrong. When he tried to move his wings, though, he couldn't. Blinding white pain shot through them again. He was somehow pinned several feet from the ground against a tall monolith in the center of what appeared to be a circular clearing, although he couldn't see fully behind him. Another slab of rock lay horizontal next to his, with a body lying on it—a dead body, wrapped in silks and surrounded by dried flowers and lines of black powder twisting and turning into symbols. The dark woods surrounded the clearing, which was bordered with a line of rocks. Torches flanked the slabs, and a fire pit flared before him. He couldn't quite place it, but something about this scene seemed familiar to him.

A large wildcat, black as night, powerfully built with corded muscles that undulated under its shiny, ebony fur, prowled in front of the fire pit. Its ears turned, and its head suddenly snapped up. Its green eyes zeroed in on Mat like laser beams. As though smiling, its lips curled upward, and its long, thick tail twitched side to side. It turned and stalked toward Mat, the firelight catching on the shiny, apple-shaped jewel hanging from its neck. Mat's heart pounded against his rib cage.

As the black panther moved toward him, it began to change. Step by step, the cat morphed into a woman. A naked woman, wearing only the necklace—the most beautiful woman Mat had ever seen.

"Shay," he tried to say, but it came out only as a soft hoot.

She stopped and looked at him, and his beak clicked. The sweet girl he'd been so attracted to did not stand before him, but the woman was definitely Shay. The light and shadows from the flames flickered and shifted over her pale face, casting it in an evil, orange glow. Her green eyes shone brightly in the dark, like a cat's. *Like a panther's*, Mathew corrected himself. *Aunt Siobhan had been right!*

"Thank you for your concern about my favorite piece of jewelry. It's made of iron, you know." Shay fingered the gem at the base of her neck. Her voice was silky smooth, just as seductive as it had been when she'd been sitting on his lap only two days ago. "You woke just in time. We have a ritual to finish."

Mat clicked and hooted, not understanding.

"Oh, yes, to *finish*," she said, as though comprehending his owlish communication. "One we started hundreds of full moons ago, but will finally end tonight with the Blood Moon. It couldn't be more appropriate. Boys?"

Two leopards came out of the darkness and strode into the circle. They each took a place on either side of Mat as Shay sauntered up to stand in front of him.

"You don't remember, do you, Mathew McFeeny?" She grinned as she leaned closer to the snowy owl, her green eyes bright. "Yes, I do know your real name. I've been tracking you for two decades, since you left that dump of an island in the Irish Sea."

Mat tried to argue with her in owl-speak. He loved Gwynf'l, his homeland, and couldn't believe anyone would call it a dump.

"Well, Gwynf'l *was* perfect, at first. For my kind. After all, it provided the seclusion we sought. We only wanted to be left to ourselves, to practice the ways of our people without tiresome interlopers. Then you came along." Shayin paused and trailed a finger along the roundness of Mat's face. "Do you believe nobody thought I could be capable of love? Not even I! But then I met someone who found a way into my cold, black heart. I thought I'd found a way into his. Even when he betrayed me . . . left me . . .

without so much as a last kiss goodbye. I've waited so long to be reunited, and here we finally are."

She paused again, and if Mat were in human form, he'd wrap her in his arms and try to make everything better for her. He wanted to tell her that he'd had no choice but to go, that his parents had said their lives were in danger. He didn't know why. He remembered nothing of what might have happened just before they left as though making an escape. He didn't remember knowing Shay before, for that matter, but he'd never tell her that. If only he could shift into his human form, explain to her what happened, and assure her that he'd meant her no grievance. He hooted and clicked again, trying to share some kind of message.

Shay pulled back. "Wait. You don't . . ." She broke into a high-pitched cackle. "You don't think I mean *you*, do you?" She sauntered past the leopard and rounded the other slab. She trailed her fingertips from the toe up along the body's wrappings until she stopped by its head. "*This* is my lover. My betrothed. My Altai." Her bright green eyes suddenly turned dangerous as her red lips curled into a snarl. "*You*, Mathew boy, are the reason he's dead!"

Mat jerked and struggled against the unseen bindings holding him against the rock. Grunts and cries emerged from his throat. How could he have killed someone? What in the hell could she be talking about?

"Oh, you didn't actually kill him. You're just the reason he's still dead. My Altai was a beautiful snow leopard, more pristine than even you, the perfect contrast to my black panther. As the daughter of the High Priestess of the Pisik Coven, I was given my choice of mates. Altai was my favorite and became my betrothed. His sexual appetite was like no other, a perfect match for me. But it was the bulbous, creamy breasts of another that was his ultimate undoing. Do you remember the merfolk of Gwynf'l, boy?"

Mat had no response. He was simply relieved to know he hadn't actually murdered another. He had a hard enough time reconciling his owl's need for meat with the killing of innocent animals, but the thought of harming a human—even if not *entirely* human—would have destroyed him.

"The merfolk of Gwynf'l are peculiar in their ability to sense inherently good and bad. Those of good nature are well rewarded, never remembering their experience, but leaving nonetheless richer. Those of the bad sort receive no such rewards. In fact, on that fateful day for my Altai, a mermaid sensed his evil sensuality and ravenously hungry instinct, and bestowed her un-reward upon my favorite lover. Altai saw Coralie from the rocks and simply couldn't stop himself. Before he turned into a human form, and without thinking —one of Altai's less admirable traits, I'll admit—he leapt in. I cannot blame him entirely. We're not exactly known for our fidelity, and I myself would probably have fallen for the swimming beauty. But as soon as Altai's paws hit the water, Coralie grabbed him and dragged him down into the cold waters. For my Altai, curiosity did kill the cat. And his death devastated me."

Shayin lifted her hand, and long, black claws grew from her fingertips. She used one to rip through the silks covering the head of the body. She pulled them away to reveal the mummified face and stroked it lovingly.

"Mother worried about me. I was her only daughter and her heir, and she promised I would grieve no longer. She met with our coven and prepared the ritual that would resurrect my Altai. The ritual was concise, and it had to occur during the Blood Moon." Shay looked up at the full moon that was just beginning its rise from behind the mountain, still large and appearing to be tainted red. "Like tonight's moon."

Shay smiled before continuing. "We gathered under the Blood Moon in a ritual circle much like this one, Mother in her full headdress with the lioness crown on her head and her black iron dagger, trimmed in rubies, in her hand." With a flick of Shay's wrist, just such a dagger appeared in her own hand. "We had the human sacrifice—a girl of virgin blood, of course—but no one else outside our circle could witness the course of events, or the ritual would be ruined. Namar and Namir here—" Shay pointed the end of the dagger at the two spotted leopards still standing sentry at Mat's sides. "—my half-brothers, roamed the forests surrounding us to ensure we were alone. We had the stone altars in place, just like this. The laying stone here." Shay gazed down at Altai's still face for a moment before striding back over to face Mat. "And the slaying stone here."

Shay's eyes narrowed as she leaned in over Mat, placing a hand on each side of his head, glaring into his round, amber eyes as though searching for the human soul within. Anyone with a keen ear could hear Mat's heart breaking. The first girl he'd ever noticed or who had ever noticed him, his first kiss, his first feel, his first hard crush, had turned out to be a monster.

"We did everything right," she snarled. "Right at sunset, when the full moon rose, Mother thrust the dagger into the girl's throat. We watched as her dark red innocence spurted like a fountain and filled the chalice I held. The fragrance was tantalizing, nearly overwhelming, but I didn't succumb to taste it. I took it to the other stone and poured the warm sanguine liquid into Altai's mouth as the coven's chants became loud and their bodies undulated to the rhythm. When they began to cry out with the intense magical energy they summoned, I took the cue and pressed my lips to my lover's cold ones. But nothing happened. He remained lifeless. Something was wrong. I screamed at my mother. I turned to my father for help. And that's when I saw the shadow of a man. But then it disappeared, and a moment later, a snow-white owl lifted into the darkening sky. Regardless of it being man or owl—or both, as it were—we had a witness."

She pulled back and lifted the dagger above her head. "But now, finally, the ritual will be complete."

CHAPTER 12

THE WINGED AND THE WICKED

Siobhan sped through the forest with Cyllene and the pixies somewhere behind. She darted one way to inspect a section before soaring back to check on them, then went off in another direction to check that way, always returning to the group. They neared Small's Falls and Peacock Lake when she saw the glow of what she knew to be firelight. Then the foul, musky odor hit her nose, and she knew they'd found Mat's captors.

"Maybe we should get Gruff first," Cyllene suggested, her voice trembling. "Seven's our lucky number, right?"

They detoured briefly to Gruff's cave, waking the troll. He grunted and groaned at the disturbance, but followed them nonetheless. The six perched in a pine tree as they waited for Gruff to catch up, and Siobhan's breath lodged in her throat when she saw the scene below them. Mathew the owl appeared to be magically bound to a stone monolith, and the shrouded body they'd seen the other day was bound on a stone slab next to him. Two leopards sat on their haunches on either side of Mat, their stench giving them away as the obnoxious, brawling brothers at the bar. Standing in front of Mat was Shayin, spilling the details of a ritual from long ago. Then she lifted the dagger above her head and proudly announced how she'd finally be able to complete the ritual to raise her lover who'd been dead for twenty-odd years.

Seeing her faerie circle defiled by such filth enraged Siobhan, but the threat to her nephew was her undoing. Like the bullet she was built to be, she became a bright white streak as she shot across the clearing.

"Except you still have witnesses!" she yelled as she cast her own magic to release Mathew from his bindings.

Shayin spun, swinging the dagger, and her fist knocked Siobhan to the ground. The leopards sprang toward her, and Namar and Namir circled the white light of the faerie who lay on her back in front of the fire pit. Mat flew up and away from the rock slab and circled overhead.

Siobhan's skin began to take on color, bubbles filling the air, and her form grew as she once again became Teeny Weeny Tahini. She began to reach into her pocket as Shayin eyed her, then the owl flying overhead. Clever enough to know what would bring him back down, the evil woman darted toward Tahini. In one quick motion, she lifted the faerie woman off the ground and hurtled her toward the giant vertical slaying stone.

Teeny, now completely effervesced to human form, hit the top of the rock. Her breathing stopped, her vision blurred, and all of her senses began to diminish at once, as she felt herself tumbling toward hell.

MAT DOVE down and caught his aunt in mid-air on her fateful fall toward the ground. The twins took clumsy swipes at the owl as he flew back up to keep out of their reach, Teeny dangling from his talons the whole time.

From somewhere above, Cyllene flew down and swirled around the tail of Namar until it caught fire. Namar let out a high-pitched scream as Cyllene darted at Namir's tail and did the same to him. The two flaming felines entered into a calamitous circling as they fervently worked to extinguish their burning wicks. While the fiery cats were consumed with their smoldering tails, Mat set the unconscious Teeny on the forest floor and flew to the circle once more to take care of the woman who'd dared to harm his beloved aunt.

Cyllene buzzed around the vile woman's head, and Shay batted at the nymph with her long-nailed, paw-like hands. One hit its mark and swatted the dryad across the circle. Cyllene hit a rock on the circle's perimeter and lay on the ground, unable to flutter a wing.

The pixies attacked next, latching onto Shayin's legs and sinking their sharp little teeth into the woman's flesh. With a kick of each leg, Shay easily shook them off, sending them soaring to join Cyllene in a big heap.

Shay shifted back into her grimalkin self, sleek and black, and in one great motion, vaulted over the rocks to where Teeny's limp body lay. Her giant paw sprung their black iron claws, and Shayin Pisik took a swipe at the immobilized fae.

Mat, furious and frightened for his loving aunt, flew toward them, but without warning, he suddenly shifted into his man-self. The strong, large figure of Mathew McFeeny landed easily on his feet and grabbed the tail of the panther, jerking her away from the helpless Teeny just in time. She swiped her sharp claws at him while he swung the bitch-cat around his head several times before letting go. Shayin, of course, landed on all fours, looked up at the bare body of Mat with her shining green eyes, and shifted into her human form. Her gaze swept over him, and her pink tongue slipped out, swiping over her lips.

"Mathew, honey, please don't hurt me," she purred as she strode toward him, swinging her hips and her naked breasts to entice him. "I've been mistaken. You and I—imagine how beautiful we can be together."

Teeny came to at that moment and saw the naked woman trying to seduce her nephew, who stood with clenched fists. She pulled the mason jar from her pocket.

"Mat!" she yelled. "Catch!"

She tossed the jar at him, and he easily caught it in his large hand. With a quick twist, he unscrewed the lid and threw the herbal dust into Shay's face. Shayin was unable to overcome her inherent cat-like nature and succumbed to the catnip. She swayed on her feet before drifting down to the ground and rolling over on her side, dazed in a pleasantly stoned state.

Meanwhile, Namar and Namir had made their way to the nearby shore of Peacock Lake and set to dousing their blazing tails. The frenzied creatures failed to realize that what seemed to them a cooling solution was an extremely noxious liquid for their kind. As their tails bobbed in and out of the water, their fur fell off their hides, leaving them hairless. Their sharp teeth dropped straight out of their gums and clattered to the ground. Their claws crumbled into eight piles of useless metal shavings. Frightened by their own reflections in the water, they ran off into the forest.

While Shay was down and stoned out of her skull, Teeny once again transformed into her faerie self and magically bound the bitch in the same way she had done to Mat. When back in her human form, Tahini retrieved a ball of wool filled with catnip from her pocket, thread a silver chain through it, and draped the chain over Shay's shoulders so the ball rest between the small cleavage of her breasts.

"That ought to keep the she-cat subdued," she said.

Mat nodded in agreement.

And then he passed out.

TEENY YELPED as her nephew collapsed in front of her, then immediately formed into an owl, lying on its side. She recalled his comment about falling out of the sky like a stuffed bird, which he resembled now.

"Oh, no, Maphew," Gruff grunted as he toddled out of the forest.

"Nice of you to show up," Teeny muttered as she circled Mat's body. She spied a long scratch down his head and the back of his neck, no doubt made by Shay's iron claw. She would need her concoction from the HOHUM book to once again draw the poison out of his system. "Watch that wretched woman," she ordered Gruff with a shake of her finger at Shay, before she hurried over to the pixies and Cyllene.

While the pixies began stirring and sitting up, Cyllene remained motionless, and her buzz had been replaced with a sad, ailing hum. "Don't worry, Silly Annie, I'll take care of you."

"She's our doc. She'll fix you right up," the pixies sang in unison.

Teeny, however, couldn't do anything for Cyllene or Mat until she first called for help. Cell phone in hand, she walked around until she finally picked up a signal. She quickly dialed 911. The phone did not ring at the fire station, nor did it ring at the sheriff's office. Tahini's 911 was her direct hotline to the mayor, who picked up immediately.

Tahini unraveled the night's events to Mayor Barbie, informing her that they had Shay subdued, but wasn't sure how long that would last. The twin leopards were still at large, but they were useless and might actually make half-decent house pets for someone now.

Tahini picked up Cyllene, cradled her in a nest of ribbons from the sisters, and tucked her into a safe place in her pocket. Just in time, too, as Sheriff Kasun arrived quite quickly with the Restraining Committee. Shay had begun to stir in the meantime, and Tahini had thrown another handful of catnip powder at her, sending her back into a mind-numbing ecstasy, drooling as she wriggled in her magical bindings.

The committee carried into the clearing a large collapsible cage and went to the task of setting it up. They had received the necessary particulars from the mayor and had brought the silver-armored cage with them, knowing it was insuperable to cat-switching witches.

The sheriff and his deputy (and son) investigated the ritual circle and the mummified body, taking notes. They inspected the supine figure of Shayin Pisik, who was currently purring in blissful idiocy.

Sheriff Ric commented to Tahini that she had done a fine job and hinted that maybe she should be on the Crime Investigation Team.

"Thank you, Sheriff, but I don't have the stomach for all this evilness," she responded truthfully.

"It's a shame those boys got away, but we'll put an APB out on them."

If Teeny didn't feel so badly about her friend in her pocket and her unconscious nephew, she might have smiled. "I don't think they'll be a problem any longer. She was the ringleader of this circus."

After transferring Shay from the floor into the cage, they closed the gate and locked it with a silver padlock. Teeny threw a sprig of catnip into the cage, "for extra measure."

The team of restrainers carried out the cage, and Ric and Conall carried out the body. Teeny watched as the imprisoned woman slowly, laboriously shifted into her black, dismal coat of fur. Before they left, Ric promised Teeny he would bring the creature before the Court of the Sun and the Moon.

Once the sheriff and the rest were gone, Teeny turned toward the pixies and Gruff.

"I need to shimmer these two to my home," Teeny told them. "You can come tomorrow if you want to check up on them. You'll be okay?"

"Gruff good," the troll said before he bumbled off toward his cave.

"The panther's gone!" Enya said.

"We're safe again!" Aeiri agreed.

"You were brave tonight," Teeny said. "Now go get some rest."

Tahini returned to her nephew's side and lifted the owl into her arms, the same as she'd done the first day she found him. She began to shimmer. This time, however, knowing Mat's true form, she rippled them into the town home's attic so he'd be more comfortable when he woke. She lay the bird in the man's bed, then went downstairs to tend to Cyllene.

She scooped the little nymph out of her pocket and lay her on the table in her laboratory-kitchen. She then gathered what she needed to make a tea, which she allowed to steep on the stovetop.

She went over to her infirm friend and placed two branches of pine on each side of her. The cleansing scent wafted through the air, and Cyllene took in a few breaths and began to recover her senses. Teeny went back to the stove and opened the drawer in the cabinet where she withdrew an eyedropper. She poured the tea into a cup and went back to Cyllene with the brew and eyedropper in hand. She placed three drops of the magical liquid onto the tiny dryad's lips, and a few seconds later Cyllene began to buzz, her wings fluttering limply, but she smiled sweetly at her idol Siobhan.

After all that happened and all of the shimmering, Teeny was exhausted, but she couldn't sleep until she knew her nephew was okay. She followed the same recipe she'd used before, but he didn't come out of it. When the sun rose, the unconscious owl transformed into a human, yet he still didn't wake.

At a loss for what else to do, she took up a vigil by his bedside until she could stay awake no longer.

CHAPTER 13

BYE-BYE BLACK CAT (FAREWELL FELONIOUS FELINE)

A loud banging on the door that led to her garden woke Teeny. She slowly lifted her head from Mat's bed, her crimped neck screaming in protest. She rolled her head, loosening the stiffness from sleeping bent over all night. The knocking became even more persistent.

"Who would have ever thought *I* would wake *you* up?" Nina asked when Tahini finally opened the back door.

The small woman blinked at her friend. "It was a very long night."

"So I heard."

Teeny lifted a brow in question.

"The mayor was at Broastful Brew when I was buying my nooner espresso, and she said a panther attacked your cabin last night, and you had to make a late-night trip home. I thought you could use this." Nina held up two cups bearing the scrawl of the Brew's logo. "Tea for you, and coffee for Mathew. I do hope he's up? I, uh, was hoping to see him."

Teeny noticed the blush creeping up Nina's neck and suppressed a smile. "He is up—but only up the stairs. I . . . I'm afraid he's ill again."

"Oh no. Well, I will go sit with him while you take a moment for yourself. Drink your tea and freshen up."

Teeny instructed Nina where to find Mathew, then sat at the table and drank her tea. She couldn't manage to stay still for long, though. She was simply too worried. So she went back upstairs, but paused at the top of the attic's ladder, finding Nina's dark head bent over her nephew. She touched her lips to Mat's head, pulled back to watch him for a moment, then drew in a deep breath before leaning down and pressing her mouth to his.

Mathew's eyelids fluttered open. He stared into the dark eyes of the Italian woman whose lips hovered above his. Then he wrapped his arms around her and pulled her down for a deeper kiss.

Tahini snuck back down the stairs with a grin nearly as wide as she was tall.

LATER IN THE AFTERNOON, they went to the cabin to prepare it for the winter snows and to visit with the sisters. When they were finished, Mat transformed into an owl, having received the power to shift at will, which Adelaide had so intuitively known to put into his tattoo ink. Teeny, feeling much relieved, effervesced and joined Cyllene and Mat on the journey home to Number 19 Main Street, flying high above the pine stand, the great falls, and the forest below them.

They arrived to find the town bustling with hoots and hollers of "Fire it up, Dragons" and other mascot-appropriate cheers for the home team. It was the night of the big game, and everyone was eager for the evening's battle. The mayor stood in the gazebo in the town square, wearing her V-necked blue and silver sweater, with a silver chain around her neck on which an elegantly crafted dragon pendant hung. The dragon's tail precariously pointed to the chasm of her bodacious breasts. She vigorously waved a pom-pom stick with blue and silver streamers in approval at the floats that circled the town square on their path to Havenwood Falls High and the glorious game that would soon begin.

The mayor had told Teeny that a special meeting of the Court of the Sun and the Moon would be held the next day, but the football game must come first. Pisik's trial would be swift, since her intended victims survived to tell their tale to the Court.

THE COURT WAS VERY fair-handed and judicious with their sentencing, but Shayin Pisik had broken too many of the town's laws. The Court ruled to have Shayin Pisik tatted by Addie for identification and obliviation, and she was banished from Havenwood Falls, sent back to the rock from which she crawled, located somewhere in the Carpathian Mountains.

The task completed, the Court wielded their swift justice, and Shayin Pisik was whisked off in a spiraling cloud of blackness, disappearing from the courtroom and the town.

Tahini invited the mayor to join her, Mat, and Cyllene at the Saloon, and the group exited the Court arm in arm, looking like Dorothy with the Lion and Tin Man, skipping down the yellow brick road. Silly Annie buzzed between the three heads that were boisterously singing the Dragons fight song.

Teeny stopped to notice a poster that had been plastered on the side of City Hall and pointed it out to her companions:

Wanted: Home For Two Adorable
RARE SPHYNX CATS,
DECLAWED AND HARMLESS

The poster depicted two hairless felines that looked remarkably like the twins after their dip in Peacock Lake.

The troupe of troubadours entered the saloon, Brent smiled his lazy warm greeting, and the three figures took seats at the bar while Cyllene rested on one of the beer taps. She sent out a few buzzes toward Brent, who knowingly fetched the funnel and kindly set it up for Madame Butterfly, his little nickname for her, since she never arrived without Madame Tahini. He never questioned how the lunar moth–like beauty could speak to them. Nina arrived and joined them, taking the seat next to Mat and scooting close enough for their shoulders to touch.

Tahini ordered a virgin pomegranate daiquiri, "with a paper umbrella, please." Mat requested his newly found favorite—a glass of Rabbit's Run. Mayor Barbie told him to surprise her, but make it strong. Barbie drank anything and everything, and could drink anyone and everyone under the table, partly because of her stature, and possibly partly through a bit of town magic. Teeny, feeling especially effervescent—in mood that was—generously offered to buy Brent a shot.

"What the hell, since it's on you, Madame." He poured himself a shot of absinthe, naturally.

They all clinked glasses, and Cyllene took the stage. She pulled out from beneath her wing her tiny lyre and strummed a couple of bars in front of the funnel spout before beginning her minstrel version of their victory:

> O yea Blood Moon had come full bloom
> And a treacherous trio entered the room
> Siobhan and Mathew felt imminent doom
> But Mat was tatted with magic injected
> Two caustic cats were soon ejected
> The vile vixen at last Mat rejected
> Mat, like a password, was safely protected.

As the mayor, Mat, Nina, and Brent began to clap exuberantly for Cyllene's performance, Tahini nearly knocked over her bar chair as she jumped to the floor.

"Oh my gods! Password! I haven't changed the town password in over two weeks." And she ran out of the saloon, leaving the batwing doors swinging behind her.

Back in her own salon, Teeny brought out her computer, opened the Havenwood Falls website, and set the new password: Ha99λ_Ha110weenλ.

~

WE HOPE you enjoyed this story in the Havenwood Falls series of novellas featuring a variety of supernatural creatures. Keep going for an excerpt of *Alpha's Queen* by Lila Felix. The series is a collaborative effort by multiple authors. Each book is generally a stand-alone, so you can read them in any order, although some authors have written sequels to their own stories. Please be aware when you choose your next read.

Havenwood Falls books by T.V. Hahn, all about Teeny Weeny and company:

The Winged & the Wicked
The Ward & the Wanderers
The Wu & the Wand

Havenwood Falls books by Kristie Cook:

Forget You Not
Lose You Not
Break Me Not
The Collector: Awakening
Savage Salvation
Sun & Moon Academy Book One: Fall Semester
Sun & Moon Academy Book Two: Spring Semester

IMMERSE YOURSELF IN the world of Havenwood Falls and stay up to date on news and announcements at www.HavenwoodFalls.com.

ABOUT THE AUTHORS

T.V. Hahn has loved the fantastical and whimsical since she was a child, which may or may not have been that long ago. A creative soul, she enjoys making art with her hands, her voice, and her words. She finds humor in everything and is the first to laugh at her own jokes. During her down time, you may find her tending her floral beauties, writing poetry, working on her faerie gardens, or watching *The Dark Crystal* or *The Princess Bride*. All of this, combined with her petite stature, has made more than one person wonder if she is, indeed, a faerie. It may be no accident that her first published book is about Teeny Weeny Tahini, a spring fae living in Havenwood Falls. Hahn is self-employed and lives in Florida with her husband and pup. She can be reached through her publisher, Ang'dora Productions.

Kristie Cook is a lifelong, award-winning writer in various genres, primarily New Adult paranormal romance and contemporary fantasy. Her internationally bestselling Soul Savers series includes seven books, as well as several companion novellas. More than 1.2 million Soul Savers books have been downloaded, hitting Amazon's, B&N.com's, and Apple's Top 100 Paid lists.

She has also written the Book of Phoenix trilogy, a New Adult paranormal romance series that includes *The Space Between*, *The Space Beyond*, and *The Space Within*. The full trilogy is available now.

Besides writing, Kristie enjoys reading, cooking, traveling, getting her hippie on, and feeding her addictions to coffee, chocolate, cheese, *The Walking Dead*, *Game of Thrones*, and *Supernatural*. She has lived in ten states, but currently calls Florida home.

Email: kristie@kristiecook.com
Author's Website & Blog: http://www.KristieCook.com
Facebook: http://www.facebook.com/AuthorKristieCook
Twitter: http://twitter.com/kristiecookauth
Goodreads: https://www.goodreads.com/KristieCook
Instagram: http://instagram.com/kristiecookauth

ACKNOWLEDGMENTS

T.V. HAHN

First and foremost, I wish to thank my co-author, publisher, and beloved niece (all one and the same) for encouraging me to take on this venture, and steering me in the right direction.

I also wish to thank my husband Paul, for patiently reading my many drafts, and reading the final edits aloud with me, and my dog Tess, who never left my side nor complained about my "story."

KRISTIE COOK

As always, thank you first to the Maker for blessing us with this life.

Thank you to my co-author and crazy aunt (we all have that one relative and I'm blessed to call T.V. Hahn mine) for being my first collaborator and joining me on this ridiculously insane adventure; for masterminding Teeny Weeny Tahini and creating the other delightful characters that have helped bring Havenwood Falls to life; and for all of your support since . . . forever. And thank you to Paul for putting up with us and contributing all you have behind the scenes.

Thank you to my sons and parents for always supporting me and listening to me gush and ramble about this fictional town, its eccentric characters, and the nearly as peculiar (and exceedingly brilliant) authors who are a part of this project.

Speaking of, thank you so much to all of the Havenwood Falls creators, current and future, who have helped make this dream a reality. Special thanks to E.J. Fechenda, Morgan Wylie, and Randi Cooley Wilson, whose creations have appeared in this book.

And we both are very grateful to our proofreader, Liz Ferry, who prevents us from being complete embarrassments to the English language. And to Regina Wamba for the *perfect* cover.

~ A Havenwood Falls New Adult Novella ~

HAVENWOOD FALLS

ALPHA'S QUEEN

LILA FELIX

Alpha's Queen (A Havenwood Falls Novella) by Lila Felix

Being the alpha's queen is the last thing Atlas Belham has ever wanted. Yet here she stands, blindfolded and binding herself to a life with a man she's never even met. All for the good of her people.

Harrison Xavier's plans have never included taking a mate, ever. He's perfectly happy to allow his cousin to assume his place as leader, especially as old feuds reignite and the Black Bear Kingdom teeters on the edge of revolution. But when he sees Atlas, his whole world shifts.

Life as a royal and in her new hometown of Havenwood Falls, where nothing is as it seems, test Atlas's resolve, but it's Harrison who tries her the most. It's ultimately up to her to choose—freedom and independence for herself or peace for the kingdom.

ALPHA'S QUEEN

AN EXCERPT

ATLAS

The lined white lace blindfold lay across the bed, mocking me. Even the bed mocked me with its pristine white coverings and golden accents along the wrought iron frame.

I wondered if this would be my bedroom—our bedroom.

"Is he that ugly? I don't get this tradition."

My best friend Samantha snickered from the corner of the room. "It would be easier to name the ones we do understand. I think this is more of a Havenwood Falls thing than a shifter thing."

"Is he ugly? Is he mean? Will he hate me? I hope he does." My voice owned a desperation I hadn't known I was capable of. At this point, I would've expected my mother to speak up and give me a few words of encouragement. As was usual for her, she remained silent, oblivious.

"You do not," Samantha said. "And even if he is ugly, you can just reap the rewards. I mean, there's the status and the money. Hell, if he's that big of a prick, you can get your needs met elsewhere, you know. I'm sure there's a yummy jester around, just waiting to make sure the future Alpha's queen is satisfied."

My best friend was not a prude, that was for sure.

"There's no jesters, Sam. This isn't the Victorian era."

She scoffed. "Could've fooled me. All these rules and that dress costs more than my rent for the year."

At least she could do that—pay her own rent. I was sure I'd never have to pay another bill while I was here. It was a little thing, but I liked the little things in life.

She was right about the dress. Swarovski crystals and pearls cluttered the lithe fabric from shoulders to hem. The style was modest to the point of almost being old fashioned. There wasn't an inch of skin from my wrists, even down to my ankles that peeked out. The lace around my collar was crowned with a string of heavy pearls. They weren't as heavy as the deal I'd made to marry a stranger.

"It isn't worth it."

She turned me around to face her. "Don't say that, Atlas. We both know what this means to our people. The classes won't be divided anymore. There won't be the rich shifters and the poor shifters. You are changing everything. Trust me, it's worth ninety days of pain and punishment." She laughed, but I did not.

I sighed and looked at myself in the mirror. I was a cinnamon bear shifter, and we were considered the lesser of the black bear shifters, even though we were technically the same species. Cinnamon bears simply didn't change from brown to white after puberty. Other than our hair color, we were the exact same bear. My lighter brown hair glistened in the sun that peeked through the moving curtains. The hairdressers had worked a full three hours on it. They didn't touch the color. It proved what I was and the reason why I was marrying the Black Bears' next Alpha.

"I don't want to change everything, Sammy. I just want to find a worthy male who loves me. I don't want to be an example or a bridge. Someone called me that the other day, by the way. They told me 'thank you for being the bridge,' like I was some inanimate thing that people walked over from one side of a dirty river to the other."

I looked in the reflection at my mother, who was already three sheets to the wind and working on the fourth. She didn't care. All she knew was the Xaviers had paid off our mortgage and my student loans—a dowry of sorts. The velvet lounge chair she rested in hugged her hips and gave her an excuse to keep chugging down the rum in her glass.

Sammy's hands were on my shoulders before the crying could start. She always knew when I was about to crack open.

"You're not an inanimate object, and anyway, I heard that Harrison is hot as fuck. And just as a bonus, he has a fine booty, too. They blindfold you so you don't slobber on him during the ceremony."

No matter how hard I tried, there was no fighting Sammy's wit. Plus, the laugh made me feel better—a little. Laughing made my breath captive in the veil that began as an adorned piece atop my head and extended below my chin. I looked like I had a fishing net stretched over my face.

Hot or not, I just wanted to be a nurse, find a mate, buy a house, and have some cubs. "This isn't right. I can't talk to people. I can't make decisions that will affect all of us. What if I fuck everything up?"

"You probably will. But, we all do, right?"

"Yeah, especially you."

"Hey! I kind of like not being perfect."

"I like you not perfect, too." I wrapped my arms around my best friend and hoped to the Creator that it wasn't the last time we would embrace like this. She'd be allowed to visit me, but only when I requested her presence.

Ninety days was all I had to last. That was the stipulation of the agreement. What would happen to the kingdom in those ninety days was beyond my knowledge, and frankly, my care. Their offer of monetary gain and peace among our people was too tempting to pass up—even if I hated every second of this set-up.

"It's not that long. I can make it, right?"

She hugged me tighter. She was crying now, too. Her body shook against me as she sobbed. "They let me meet him last night, At."

I pulled back, shocked by her confession. "What the hell? Why didn't you tell me? I was wondering how you knew what he looked like. I thought you were just trying to make me feel better."

"They told me not to. But I couldn't keep it from you. He's...he's not what you think. That's all I'm going to say. You won't have any trouble lasting the ninety days. Treat this like a real mating. Trust me."

I did.

I just didn't trust my mate-to-be.

A knock sounded at the door. A pith of a girl with a pale pink dress told us that it was almost time. Almost time to go.

"Well, let's not drag this out." Sammy reached to straighten my veil again and kissed me on the cheeks.

"One day maybe . . ."

"Don't even say it, Atlas. It's just a few days, and then you will be free of this place."

I fisted the sleeve of her dress, not willing to let her go yet.

"All of this is ridiculous. This castle. This wedding. This dress. These rules. What kind of Alpha won't let my best friend attend my wedding?"

"It's all about numbers, Atlas. You know that. Your mom will be there along with some servants. That many cinnamon bears under one roof is probably making the Alpha squirm enough without adding one more to the mix."

She stepped away but before her hand touched the door, she looked over her shoulder at me. "You have to change things, Atlas. At the very least, you have to try."

The girl who had summoned me still stood at the door, staring at me as though I'd just given birth to an alien. "Is something wrong?" I asked, checking myself over in the mirror.

"No, ma'am. Is it true? You've come to help us?" Her question was barely audible.

Sammy and I looked at each other in shock. My stomach rolled as I realized the shake in this girl's voice wasn't from speaking to me, but rather what she eluded to.

"I'm going to try."

Try was the only thing I could promise.

HARRISON

Every time my father, the Alpha, paced from one side of the room to another, he took a glance at himself in the mirror. It was like watching the most conceited ballerina on the planet.

"Dad, could you please stop? You're making me nervous and frankly driving me bat . . . just crazy."

He tossed a look over his shoulder telling me not only would he not stop, but that I'd better shut up about it as well. I learned that look at an early age.

"We have to make this work, Harrison. The people—the lesser ones—they are making it hard on us. They reject our decisions. They resist. We have to earn their trust again or our dynasty is in jeopardy. I'm not sure you're taking this seriously enough."

What my father didn't understand was that I didn't give a fuck if the dynasty fell down around us and burned to the ground. The only thing I had my sights set on was waiting out my father's reign to end. Whether it be by death or by old age, he would have to give up on his tyranny one day, and even if he did offer me the position of Alpha, which he would not, I would not accept. I was content to allow Dolrich to take my place as his shadow, hoping that my father would favor him in place of me. Dolrich would be our new Alpha, even if my father didn't quite grasp it yet.

Not that he really favored me all that much in the first place.

A knock at the door finally stopped my father from pacing and made me immediately stand at attention. This was it. It was time for me to be married to someone I didn't know.

Ridiculous. All of it.

"It's just me. Stand down." Dolrich opened the door and closed it behind him quickly. He was wearing a similar tux to mine except my tie and handkerchief were gold, signifying my rank as in line for Alpha. His was purple, which showed he was royalty.

I knew that my new mate would be wearing a gold garter underneath her pristine white dress.

Hey, I had to get happy about something in this disastrous day.

"Dolrich, you scared the f...you scared me."

The Alpha didn't appreciate vulgar language in his presence. Too bad fuck was my favorite word. Last time I said damn in front of him, he reached over and covered my mother's ears. She didn't even blink an eye. Mother's favorite word was ass.

Dolrich bared his neck a little for the intrusion. "Sorry. I came to wish you luck. I've heard she's a looker. They are almost ready for you."

A looker. Sometimes looks were just not enough.

My dad bowed up. It seemed he took offense at everything anyone said lately, and my cousin wasn't immune to his defensiveness. "You think I would choose anything less for the next Alpha? His queen must be honorable and beautiful."

One of Dolrich's eyebrows raised at me. Dad was insane. Plus, I gave zero fucks about being the next Alpha. Any other eligible male could have it. Hell, any of my brothers could have this female I was supposed to be joined to in the next hour. It was a stiff and cold coupling just like anyone else's in this family.

Royals didn't marry for love. They married for position, or in my case, I was being married off for political leverage. My father's attitude and general orders that looked down at the lesser bears of our species were earning him some backlash in the last decade or so. He thought marrying me off to one of them would balm their wounds.

He might be right.

He might be off his fucking rocker.

"Of course not, Alpha. I was simply trying to ease my cousin's nerves a little. He's practically shaking," Dolrich replied.

Was not.

My dad crossed his arms over his chest. "There's nothing for him to be nervous about. Alphas don't get nervous. We stand up and get things done. This isn't emotional. It's his duty."

Another knock came at the door. This time all three of us squared our shoulders for the event to come. I knew it was one of the servants before they even spoke.

"It's time, Alpha."

My father nodded once. Thad, my father's private butler, shut the door with a bow.

"Dolrich, do you mind if I have a word with my son before the ceremony? It will be quick. Please tell everyone that we will be there shortly."

Dolrich bowed a little. "Of course, Alpha. Good luck, Harrison."

The bastard winked at me.

I rolled my eyes at him.

As soon as the door was shut, the Alpha was in front of me in the body that used to be my father. He was stiff again. His voice grew cold. His eyes emptied. His jaw clenched.

"This is the day you begin your role as the future Alpha. Taking this female is your promise to keep those other bears in line. It is a sacrifice, I know, but it has to be done. We can't have an uprising on our hands. There will be time to mate with her, but the blood rites must be done tonight. You understand? I won't be embarrassed by an unmarked daughter-in-law. Is that clear? I mean it this time, Harrison. I realize you don't have the strength or the gumption to become the Alpha I am, but at least you could put on the façade of one. I shouldn't even have to tell you this. You are my son. This should come to you like breathing."

Though everything in me wanted to buck against his system, I bared my neck in respect. "Yes, Alpha. I understand my duty."

"Well, blind obedience will do in the absence of true loyalty for the meantime. You need to make a decision while you are up there securing a future for yourself with this marriage. Dolrich is tough and commanding, unlike you. If not for me, he would've challenged you to a fight for the future seat as Alpha already. I was giving you a chance to become what you were born to be. While you are taking this—" he flicked his hand in the air "—mate today, think about who it is that will take my place when I am gone. Think very hard if you want to give up on your legacy—the legacy of your family."

There was nothing to think about. The choice was already made.

Purchase *Alpha's Queen* at your favorite book retailer.

www.ingramcontent.com/pod-product-compliance
Lightning Source LLC
Chambersburg PA
CBHW052007170626
46808CB00007B/2820